Cornish Mystery

Cornish Mystery

Jean Bellamy

Marshall Pickering

Pickering and Inglis
Marshall Pickering
3 Beggarwood Lane, Basingstoke, Hants RG23 7LP, UK

Copyright © 1986 by Jean Bellamy

First published in 1986 by Pickering and Inglis Ltd
Part of the Marshall Pickering Holdings Group
A subsidiary of the Zondervan Corporation

All rights reserved. No part of this publication may be reproduced, stored in a retrieval system, or transmitted, in any form or by any means, electronic, mechanical, photocopying, recording or otherwise, without the prior permission in writing, of the publisher.

British Library CIP Data

Bellamy, Jean
  Cornish mystery.
  I. Title
  823'.914[J]   PZ7

ISBN: 0-7208-0691-7

Text set in Plantin by Brian Robinson, North Marston, Bucks.
Printed and bound in Great Britain by Hazell Watson & Viney Ltd, Member of the BPCC Group, Aylesbury, Bucks.

Contents

1:	Sheba	7
2:	In the Enemy Camp	18
3:	Danger!	27
4:	A Miracle	36
5:	Rescued	42
6:	God's Mighty Army	48
7:	Who are the two men?	55
8:	Another Fright	64
9:	Lost and Found	74
10:	The Mystery Deepens	81
11:	Tessa Learns the Truth	91
12:	Where are the Twins?	99
13:	Tessa to the Rescue	108
14:	Home Again	120

1: Sheba

It was a swelteringly hot August afternoon. Not a cloud was to be seen in the clear blue sky as Tessa walked slowly along the cliff path. She had never been to Cornwall before and she certainly hadn't wanted to come – though the twins had been quite looking forward to it. Yet now, as she looked at a big black-headed gull screeching defiantly at her from the tall, craggy cliffs, and the sea sparkling and glinting in the sunlight, it didn't seem quite so bad after all.

Which was just as well, thought Tessa, considering she and the twins had got to spend the whole of their summer holidays with Uncle George and Aunt Jane in their little bungalow on the outskirts of the village. All the same, it was going to be pretty dull and boring, after they had been looking forward for months to a holiday in Switzerland – their first holiday abroad – and she kicked at a stone with her sandalled foot and suddenly realised that Peter and Paula were nowhere to be seen.

'Bother!' she muttered and stopped in the middle of the narrow path to look back, shading her eyes with her hand. Then she saw them some way behind, crouched much too near the edge of the cliff, picking wild flowers.

'Come on you two,' she shouted; at twelve she was four years older than they were, and was expected to keep an eye on them. 'It's your turn to carry the beach bag, and if you don't, you won't get any tea.' The children sprang to their feet and came scurrying towards her, rushing past with whoops of delight.

'Come on slow-coach!' Peter yelled as he flashed past, dragging his twin by the hand and Paula called over her shoulder that the tide looked just right for a swim and they didn't care about tea anyway!

Tessa frowned and glared after them. Then she too broke into a run, her feet sinking into the springy turf covered with sea-pinks. Ahead there was a crescent-shaped gap in the cliffs and she knew that hundreds of feet below lay a tiny cove. The twins were nearly there, rushing headlong towards the cliff edge, red hair gleaming in the sunshine. Tessa's heart beat a little quicker, for the steps cut in the rock-face were very steep and uneven, and Uncle and Auntie had warned them all, as soon as they had arrived three days ago, that they mustn't take risks or do anything silly.

'Race you down the steps, Paula!'

As Peter's piping tones wafted back to Tessa, she shouted, 'Wait for me!' and to her relief they did, but not without a lot of grousing and arm-waving. She was just about to join them when a sound caught her ears and she stopped once more, standing stockstill and looking over to her left. Was it her imagination, or had she heard a faint cry like an animal in pain, coming from the big field on the other side of the low stone wall, where hundreds of woolly sheep cropped the rich green grass? She held her breath, straining her eyes and ears, but there was nothing to be heard now, except the cry of a gull drifting lazily overhead with its wings stretched out, and the quiet lap of the sea in the background. Yet there *had* been something, she was sure, and next moment it came again and this time there was no doubt about it. So she looked back at the twins, who were hopping about impatiently and demanding to know why she couldn't get a move on, and pointed in the direction of the field.

'I can hear something over there! It sounds like a dog in pain! I'm going to have a look.'

There were more groans from the twins as she made for the wall, but Paula who liked to be in on everything called out, 'Wait for me Tess!' and sprinted after her sister who was already scrambling over into the field.

There was quite a deep ditch on the other side, but swinging her long legs, Tessa landed safely, and the next moment a couple of human whirlwinds thudded up behind her. Unfortunately the twins didn't look where they were going, and launched themselves into space right into the middle of a big patch of stinging nettles and brambles on the other side.

'Ouch! I've been stung all over,' Paula wailed, whilst Peter, eyes screwed up because the sun was in them, scowled and scratched furiously at his bare arms and legs. The sheep, woolly sides heaving with fright, took themselves off to the other end of the field, and from a safe distance they stared back at the intruders with frightened expressions on their timid faces.

'There's nothing here, silly,' Peter said scornfully. 'Stupid old Tess!' Paula added. But as if to contradict them, there came an unmistakeable whimper from another big clump of nettles further along the wall and the twins looked excited as Tessa darted forward and knelt on the ground to peer into the long lank undergrowth. Then she turned and beckoned eagerly to them.

'It *is* a dog,' she said triumphantly.

'A . . . a sort of black spaniel . . .' Peter murmured wonderingly as he stared over her shoulder. 'I wonder what's wrong with him!'

'Isn't he lovely,' said Paula, dropping to her knees beside Tessa.

The spaniel lay in a crumpled heap amongst the nettles and Tessa parted them gingerly, stretching out one hand to touch the black, silky head.

'Will he bite?' Peter asked nervously.

'' Course not, silly,' Tessa told him irritably. 'Spaniels don't bite.'

'They do sometimes!' he retorted, not unreasonably. 'Especially when they're hurt.'

But the dog only gazed up at them all with big, soft brown eyes which seemed full of pain. Paula edged nearer and ran her fingers along the smooth back and feathered legs, whereupon the spaniel whimpered again and looked pleadingly at the children.

'He probably hurt himself falling into the ditch. I expect he jumped the wall,' Tessa said, and her young sister's blue-green eyes grew round like saucers as she pushed her untidy auburn hair back from her hot face.

'He's got a collar on anyway. And there's a disc on it . . .'

Peter, who sometimes had trouble with his vocabulary, stared thoughtfully at the injured spaniel and said, 'He's not been disbanded then, or he wouldn't be wearing one, would he?'

'Abandoned,' Paula corrected with a look of scorn, and suddenly the spaniel was struggling to get up, long plumed tail waving slowly from side to side, only to fall back again with a cry of distress. At that moment, Paula, who had been trying to read the writing on the disc, gave a shout of triumph and sat back on her heels.

'His name's Sheba,' she announced importantly.

'Sheba's a girl's name, stupid,' retorted Peter, quick to get his own back. 'It's a she, not a he,' he told her loftily.

'Oh all right, Mr Cleversticks,' Paula pouted, and as the two younger children glared at one another, Tessa said crossly, 'Oh, do stop arguing, both of you. We've got to get help from somewhere. Sheba can't stand, let along walk . . . Is there an address on the disc, Paula?'

'Let *me* look!' Peter leant forward and gave his twin a little push that toppled her over. 'Yes, there is! On the other side! It says . . . No. 2 Coastguard Cottages.'

'That's *miles* away,' Paula frowned, recovering her balance.

'It's *not*. It's only about one mile, I should think,' Peter retorted.

'That's still too far for us to carry her,' Tessa sighed, and flicked her long fair hair out of her eyes, for it was getting hotter and the twins more argumentative every minute. 'Anyway, I should think it's more like two miles, because they're way out on those tall cliffs close by that big headland. Uncle pointed them out to us the day before yesterday when we went for that walk.' She looked down at the dog again and stroked her long silky fur. 'It's a good thing you've got a nice thick coat, Sheba, or you'd be stung all over, lying in that nasty bed of nettles. We can't move you, I'm afraid. You're much too heavy.'

'We'll have to get help, won't we?' Paula was looking thoughtful for once. 'We can't just leave her . . .'

''Course not, silly,' put in Peter, and Tessa butted in quickly before they started rowing again.

'Tell you what, I'll stay here with Sheba while you two go and fetch somebody. If you can't find anyone on the cliffs, you'll just have to go back home and ask Uncle to come. She needs a drink badly though – so hurry!'

The matter settled – though Tessa was not quite sure that she ought to let the twins go wandering off on their own – she bent over the spaniel again. Perhaps she should have suggested going herself, but she didn't like to leave Sheba with Peter and Paula. They were just as likely – knowing them – to get fed up with waiting and go off to the beach or something. In fact, Peter was already beginning to look a bit bored.

'We shan't get our bathe,' he grumbled, but Paula was jumping around excitedly, tired of hanging around and anxious to be off.

'Oh come on, Coppernob, let's go,' she said impatiently,

and before he could object, she had grabbed him by the arm and was propelling him towards the wall. Tessa watched them go, smiling to herself at the way Peter said, 'Coppernob yourself!' And sitting on the hard ground beside the injured spaniel, she saw the two sturdy redheads clamber over to the other side, and could only hope they didn't get into any mischief.

They hadn't gone more than a few yards however, when to her surprise, she saw them stop dead in their tracks and look at each other in dismay. Then they were staring back at her uncertainly, and at the same time she became aware of the sound of voices in the distance, and singing mingled with laughter, which seemed to be getting louder every minute.

Jumping to her feet and shading her eyes with her hand, she looked in the direction from which it was coming, and there along the cliff path a crowd of people was swinging into view. They were coming rapidly nearer – thirty or more chattering boys and girls with two grown-ups bringing up the rear – and she knew at once who they were. It was the 'beach mission lot' as she and the twins had christened them, and it hadn't taken them long to make up their minds what they thought of *them*! So not surprisingly, she felt as alarmed as Peter and Paula, but getting help was more important than anything else at that moment, and she sent urgent signals to the twins. For she was afraid that if they didn't do something quickly, Sheba who was lying very still now with her eyes closed, might die of pain and thirst. But the next moment, to her annoyance, the children were thudding back towards her, with looks of disgust on their faces.

'It's those people! We can't ask *them*, Tessa,' Peter said, and Paula muttered, 'They probably won't want to help anyway. They're treasure-hunting, I expect, or whatever they do.'

'What does that matter, for goodness' sake?' Tessa asked

crossly. 'They won't eat you, sillies. And if they go to church, then they jolly well ought to help us.' And taking a deep breath, she sprinted over the wall and broke into a run, the twins at her heels.

The group was moving at quite a fast pace along the cliff path, and Tessa was afraid they might go by before she could stop them. So she called out breathlessly and a little nervously, 'I say, can you help us, please!' and those nearest the back stopped and turned round. Then the whole crowd were standing looking at them, and the trio felt suddenly shy and self-conscious at being faced with such a lot of people. They waited, hearts thudding, as one of the two grown-ups came striding towards them; and as he got closer, they could see that he was tallish and not all that old.

'Trouble?' he asked as he came up to them, and Tessa thought, rather grudgingly, that close to he didn't look bad, after all.

'Yes. We . . . we wondered if you could help us. We've found a dog over in that field. He . . . she seems to have hurt her paw.' Tessa turned to point back over the wall behind them. 'She's much too heavy for us to carry . . . and we don't know what to do . . .'

'She might die,' put in Peter, worriedly scuffing the ground with his sandals and looking bashfully at the stranger, whilst Paula stared at him unblinkingly and added, 'Of thirst.'

'Right then.' Tessa saw a glint of amusement in the stranger's eyes, but his voice was friendly enough. 'I'll be with you in a moment,' he said and called out 'Sally!' to the person he had been walking with, and hurried back to speak to her.

'Come along then!' he said when he returned to them. 'Let's have a look at the little chap,' and he gave them an encouraging smile. So Tessa and the twins fell into step beside him, Peter murmuring that it wasn't a he but a she!

'Her name's Sheba,' added Paula, 'and she's all black and bigger than an ordinary spaniel.'

'Do you know about dogs?' Peter asked rather doubtfully. But Tessa said nothing at all, for she didn't much like the way things were going, and she certainly didn't intend to get too friendly—though really there was nothing else they could have done, she told herself.

'A little!' Their companion's eyes were twinkling again. 'I've got two of my own, you see!'

'Oh!' The twins both spoke at once and looked surprised. Then all four of them were clambering over the wall and Tessa was leading the way to where Sheba lay amongst the nettles. Hearing them, the spaniel opened her long-lashed eyelids and looked up, and Tessa remembered that they hadn't told the stranger where she lived.

'Her address is on the disc on her collar,' she said. 'It's No.2 Coastguard Cottages.'

'Good! . . . I say, what a lovely dog!' He stooped and parted the nettles, stroking Sheba's head and turning to the children again. 'We haven't introduced ourselves yet, have we! I'm Steve.' He had such a nice smile that when he looked at Tessa and said, 'And you're . . .?' she felt she almost liked him.

'I'm Tessa,' she told him, 'and the twins are Peter and Paula.'

'Fine!' He looked down at the spaniel again. 'Now Sheba lass,' he said soothingly, 'we'll have you home in no time,' and without wasting another moment, he knelt beside her and ran his hand gently over her injured hindleg. 'No. 2 Coastguard Cottages,' he repeated thoughtfully. 'They're up on the headland, aren't they? I should be able to carry her,' and he slipped one hand beneath Sheba's head and the other under her back. Then he lifted her carefully and straightened up, watched eagerly by the children, and she lay in his arms, eyes closed again.

'Is she heavy?' Tessa asked anxiously.

'Not too bad, Tessa. I'll take her home straight away. I'm not sure about that leg. Looks as though it could be painful, and I think she ought to see a vet as soon as possible.'

They moved off, and Steve handed Sheba to Tessa whilst he climbed over the wall. Then she gave her back to him and climbed over herself, followed by the twins. Once over the wall there was a short pause during which the three children stood awkwardly in a bunch.

'Er ... thank you very much,' Tessa said at last, remembering her manners. And that should have been the end of it, but as they started to walk away, Steve called after them, 'Well done, all of you! You've certainly done your good deed for the day. You're on holiday, I take it?'

Tessa turned and nodded, aware that now it was all over, the twins had lost interest and were looking longingly towards the beach.

'We're staying with my Uncle and Aunt in the village,' she told him, and suddenly she didn't want to go until she knew Sheba was safely home. So rather to her surprise she heard herself saying, 'Do you think I could come with you and Sheba?' thinking to herself as she said it that if the twins didn't want to come too, they could jolly well go off on their own. It was obvious they didn't, for Paula said 'What about our bathe?' in a voice that was meant to be a whisper but wasn't, and Peter said equally loudly that it would be much too late by the time they got back, as the tide would have come right in, and they couldn't go on their own!

So Tessa just shrugged and was silent – though she pulled a face at the twins and hoped Steve, who was looking rather thoughtful, wouldn't notice. Then suddenly he was speaking again.

'Look, tell you what! Tessa can come with Sheba and me, and Peter and Paula can join our group. They'll be down in the cove by now and they're all going in for a swim. You'll be there in two minutes if you hurry. Just tell Sally that I sent you along, and she'll be delighted to have you both. They're a friendly lot, you'll find.'

The twins looked at each other doubtfully and Tessa, unable to make up her mind whether she wanted them to go or not, frowned at them again. For half an hour ago, the last thing any of them would have thought of doing was to join in with the 'beach mission lot'. Yet if Peter and Paula didn't do as Steve had suggested, she would have to take them to the beach herself, and then she wouldn't be able to see Sheba safely home. It was all very difficult, for Steve was standing there waiting for them to make up their minds.

'All right, we'll go,' Paula murmured after a silence that seemed to go on and on, and Peter nodded slowly, staring doubtfully at his twin. Then he looked at Tessa and muttered that it was all her fault anyway, though if Steve heard, he showed no sign of it. After which the twins clasped hands firmly for mutual support and, having grabbed the beach bag from Tessa, set off at a trot towards the beach.

Steve called out after them. 'Goodbye twins, and enjoy yourselves,' and Tessa, glancing sideways at him as they walked off in the opposite direction saw that twinkle in his eyes again.

For a few minutes Steve didn't speak, and Tessa kept looking at Sheba and wondering whether she was going to be all right. For her eyes were tightly closed now and she looked a bit limp – though quite contented – as she lay in Steve's arms with her head resting on his shoulder.

'What's your other name, Tessa?' asked Steve, breaking the silence.

'Grant,' she told him briefly, for alone with him she felt suddenly shy and tongue-tied – and besides, in spite of the fact that he had turned out to be not as bad as she would have expected, she still didn't want to have anyting to do with him and his crowd, for she was on holiday and meant to enjoy herself.

'Have you been here before?'

'No,' Tessa told him. 'Never. Auntie and Uncle have only just moved here from London.' She sighed and went on, 'We *were* going to Switzerland on a package holiday, but Mummy and Daddy had a bad car accident a few weeks ago and are in a nursing home convalescing. We haven't ever been abroad, and we'd been looking forward to it for ages – and then we had to come here instead,' she finished miserably, and she knew she sounded fed up and sorry for herself.

Perhaps Steve guessed that she was rather sad about it all too, for he said quickly, 'That must have been disappointing for you, and I'm so sorry about your parents,' but she stared away from him down the cliff to the big sandy beach below where the tide was on the turn. Only yesterday morning she and the twins had seen the big red banner and the sand pulpit on this very beach, and the large crowd of boys and girls gathered round singing hymns and songs and reading from the Bible, and she had thought it very odd – certainly not the sort of thing *she* would want to do – particularly in front of all those holidaymakers enjoying themselves on the beach.

As she didn't speak, for she was miles away, Steve shifted the dog in his arms to a more comfortable position and followed her gaze. Tessa froze at his next words.

'As you probably know, I'm helping to run a beach mission here, and we meet down there at Poltuan Beach every morning from Monday to Friday, ten-thirty to eleven-thirty.' He paused and added, 'We'd love it if you and the twins could join us!'

2: In the Enemy Camp!

Tessa didn't answer, and she would have given anything at that moment to be able to run away. Which was silly, of course, for Steve seemed quite nice really. So after an awkward pause – at least Tessa felt awkward – he went on as though he hadn't noticed that anything was wrong: 'We do other things too, like the beach party this afternoon, and playing cricket and rounders and things. And there are treasure-hunts, and we go surfing every morning after the beach service. Oh – and there's going to be a barbecue on the beach next Saturday evening.'

Tessa had to be polite and say something, so she murmured that she would have to ask Uncle and Auntie first, and Steve said, 'Of course,' and went on to tell her that they would all be meeting at about 10.15 tomorrow morning – which was Sunday – to go to the service at the little old church on the cliff-top not far away.

'Do come along if you can – think about it anyway!'

Tessa was silent again, wracking her brains for an excuse, but she couldn't think of anything. So she looked towards the beach once more, where the tide was flowing in quite quickly over the broad stretch of golden sand, to where she could see the entrances to several big caverns in the cliff-face. Her heart beat a little faster as she thought how exciting it would be to explore them. Then she looked at the huge waves rolling up the beach – all froth and foam – and the bathers enjoying themselves in the surf, and she wanted more than anything to have a surf-board and learn to use it, but Uncle and Auntie had absolutely forbidden her and the twins to go surfing on their own. It could be very dangerous, they said, and one had to take notice of the warning flags placed along the beach. It was easy to get caught in the currents and get swept out to sea and drowned. It wasn't safe to go in at all, in fact, when the red flag was flying, Uncle had said.

And now she was being invited to go surf-bathing with the beach party – and oh! how she would have loved to go. But of course she couldn't, for that would mean going to the service first, and sitting in rows in front of the sand pulpit under the big red banner, singing hymns, and she had no intention of doing *that*. So, to change the subject, she looked quickly at Sheba and said that she hoped her paw wasn't broken.

'Oh, I don't think so, Tessa. Just badly sprained, I expect.' And then he started asking her what her hobbies were, and forgetting her shyness she chatted quite happily until suddenly the Coastguard Cottages were in front of them, standing stark and white and lonely on the gaunt headland, miles from anywhere.

'Here at last!' her companion said cheerfully. 'I'll run you back in my car as soon as we've dropped Sheba off. Then you can join the twins and the rest of them on the beach.'

Tessa turned away with a frown and bit her lip, and started thinking about Peter and Paula again and wondering how they were getting on, right in the enemy camp! Then she looked again at the three whitewashed buildings and was glad they were there at last.

The cottages looked quite old with their thick walls and small windows, and each one had a little garden in front, though nothing much was growing in the beds around the lawns. Sheba must have realised she was home at last, for she raised her head suddenly, showing signs of life, and as Steve hadn't got a free hand, Tessa pushed open the gate of

No. 2 and they walked up the narrow path to the front door. Tessa pressed the bell and they didn't have long to wait, for in a few moments a woman with dark hair and eyes appeared, wearing a worried look on her face as she looked at her visitors. But next moment her eyes lit up with relief!

'Oh! . . . There she is! We've been so worried,' she told them breathlessly, opening the door wide. 'We thought she might have fallen over the cliff and got killed. Where did you find her?' she asked eagerly.

Steve handed Sheba over and explained to her mistress — her name was Mrs Jenkins, she said — the part Tessa and the twins had played in the afternoon's little drama, adding that it was fortunate he had been coming by just at the right moment. 'I'm Steve Michelmore, by the way,' he said, 'and this is Tessa Grant,' he added, and pushed her forward.

'Thank you so much Tessa! And you too, Mr Michelmore, for carrying her all this way. Come in both of you,' and she led the way into a small sitting-room opening off to the right of the tiny hallway. When they were sitting down, she went out of the room and came back with a bowl of water, which Sheba lapped thirstily as she lay on the floor, after which the spaniel seemed to revive a little. Steve explained about her paw, and Mrs Jenkins examined it and agreed that it would be a good idea to let the vet see it though when she pulled a big dog-basket out from under the table, Sheba actually got up and limped into it.

'My husband and son and I have been so worried,' she said again, 'and I hope they won't be too long coming back, for they've been out for quite a while now, scouring the cliffs. It's a wonder you didn't meet them, but perhaps they've gone the other way. Sheba does wander about a lot on her own,' she went on, 'but usually we don't worry because she's lived here since she was a tiny puppy. She's usually very sure-footed and used to climbing the cliffs. I suppose she twisted her leg when she jumped the wall into that ditch, as you suggested.'

They chatted a while longer and then Steve stood up and said they must be getting along. Tessa got up too, though rather reluctantly, for now that the time had come for her to part company with Sheba, she didn't want to go. So she knelt down on the rug beside her basket and gave the spaniel a hug, and just at that moment they all heard the click of the gate through the open window, followed by footsteps on the path.

'Here they are,' said Mrs Jenkins, and next minute a middle-aged man, tanned and weatherbeaten, and a tall boy a little older than Tessa with thick brown curly hair and a friendly smile, walked into the room. Their faces lit up when they saw Sheba in her basket. 'I'm so glad you're back!' said Mrs Jenkins, and introduced her visitors, explaining what had happened.

To Tessa's surprise, Steve and her son, whose name was David, seemed to know one another already, and David said, 'This is Steve from the Beach Mission,' and his father and mother both smiled and seemed pleased to meet him.

Steve and Tessa were warmly thanked again and after a little more conversation, Steve said he thought they ought to be getting along. Finally, they all said 'goodbye', Steve reminding David as they left – to Tessa's surprise – that he would see him at church tomorrow morning. With a final wave, he and Tessa set off in the direction of the main road.

'We haven't got very far to go,' Steve told her as they walked along, but Tessa had other things on her mind at that moment. Fancy David being one of the Beach Mission lot – she wouldn't have thought it of him! But she didn't have long to dwell upon it, for suddenly they had reached the main road, and in front of them was a big square house built of Cornish granite.

'Our headquarters!' Steve said with a smile, and before Tessa could object, he was leading her towards a rather ancient, battered car which stood just outside the gate. He opened the door of the passenger seat for her, and because she couldn't think of any excuse not to, she found herself climbing in beside him. Then they were off and she really was rather glad to sit down for she was feeling very hot and tired.

But as they bumped back towards Trewinth along a rough track, she began to hope that the tide would be right in, so that everyone would have had to come up from the beach and she could go home with the twins. But when they got there and looked over the edge, she could see that it was only half way up and there were quite a lot of people there still. All the same, she couldn't help feeling a little bit excited, for the tiny sandy cove, surrounded on three sides by towering cliffs, fascinated her. There were nice flat slabs of rock and small rock pools full of seaweed and anemones, and tiny fish and crabs. The rocks were all covered with mussels and limpets, though when she and the twins had tried to pull the limpets off, they had found they only clung on all the harder, so that it was impossible to move them unless you were very quick.

Then she came back to earth again, for Steve said, 'There they are!' and following his pointing finger, she saw them all, on the right hand side under the cliff. There was nothing for it but to clamber down the steps with Steve, and walk across the firm sand weaving in and out between the sunbathers. As they got nearer to the group, she could see that some of them were digging an enormous sandcastle, whilst others were sitting about on the rocks eating sandwiches and drinking bottles of pop. Steve introduced her to Sally, the person he had been walking with on the cliff top earlier on.

'Hello Tessa,' Sally said kindly, and asked her how the dog was. Then she patted the rock beside her and Tessa sat down and looked around for the twins. She soon spotted them, running up and down the beach with some children of their own age, and to her surprise they looked as though they were thoroughly enjoying themselves. She felt terribly let down – surely they hadn't gone over to the enemy already, she thought anxiously! She couldn't believe *that* of them!

To cover her annoyance, she busied herself getting sandwiches and cake out of the beach-bag which was lying nearby with the twins' clothes, and she munched in silence, listening to Sally chatting to Steve, who had just joined them. Now and again they spoke to her, trying to draw her into the conversation. While she was eating Peter and Paula rushed towards her and told her they were having an absolutely super time! She felt like telling them off, but of course she couldn't with Steve and Sally and all the others around. A game of rounders seemed about to begin and the twins tore off excitedly to help with knocking the stumps into the sand. A girl with long plaits who said her name was Melanie, asked Tessa if she was going to come and join in.

'I don't think so,' Tessa said, shaking her head. But Melanie looked a bit disappointed, which made her feel rather mean. So she changed her mind and said, 'All right, but I'm not much good at rounders.' Melanie said neither was she, and it didn't matter.

They walked over to where the others were taking up their positions, but after about ten minutes she wished she had said 'no'. She wasn't really thinking what she was doing and missed the ball so many times when it came her way that the others had to keep running into the sea after it, and she thought they must all be feeling fed up with her.

At last it was over and everyone was getting ready for a last dip. Tessa changed quickly into her swimsuit feeling much happier now, for she was quite a good swimmer and loved it. Leaving Melanie and the others behind, she ran straight into the sea and struck out, keeping parallel with the rocks which ran out on the right of the cove and divided

Trewinth from the next bay. She had seen this other beach already from the cliff-top, and like Trewinth it had fascinated her, though for a different reason. It was also sandy, but much, much bigger and very long. But more important, there seemed to be no way down to it from the cliff, so that when the tide was coming in, it was completely deserted except for the gulls and other sea-birds, although at low tide you could walk round the corner to it from Trewinth.

The further she swam, the quieter it became for she could no longer hear the others calling to each other, and suddenly she was far enough out to be able to see the next beach. She could see something else too which she hadn't noticed from the top of the cliff — a big yawning hole in the craggy cliff-face which she knew was a cave. She had just made up her mind that she would walk round to it one day when the tide was low, when she became aware of voices and shouting coming from the beach a long way behind her. Startled, she looked over her shoulder towards the shore, where she could see Steve and Sally and some of the others, standing at the water's edge, waving her in.

She saw something else too, which was that she was a long way out — much further than she had thought. But she wasn't frightened, not even when she looked down into the clear green water at the sea-bed far below, and realised that she was right out of her depth.

'I had better go in though,' she supposed, so she turned and started swimming leisurely towards the beach, surprised that she seemed to be causing such a commotion. She *was* feeling a bit tired by the time she reached the shallow water, and as she walked out onto the hot, firm sand, she was uncomfortably aware that everyone was standing around looking at her. What a fuss to make about nothing, she thought, and quite forgot what Auntie and Uncle had told her about the currents! Steve hurried towards her, with

Sally close behind, both looking rather serious. 'We thought you were trying to swim to America, or something Tessa,' he said, but she didn't laugh because she knew he wasn't really joking. 'It's better to keep with the others and not to go out too far,' he went on in a quiet voice which only she and Sally could hear. 'Even if the tide *is* coming in,' and the way he said it made her feel as though she had done something very silly. So she just nodded casually and said 'OK,' though she thought they were making an awful to-do about nothing. It wasn't as though the sea was rough, and she didn't like being treated like a child. Then she walked away with her head in the air, and towelled herself dry in the hot sun, a little apart from the others, feeling warm and glowing after her swim. What had just happened had made her even more determined to keep away from these people, and she started thinking about the beach round the corner again.

Then she noticed that the tide was beginning to flow in quite fast, and that everyone was packing up to go. So stuffing her things into the beach bag, she walked slowly towards the steps a little behind the others – glad that it was all over at last – when Melanie who was just in front of her, turned round and waited.

'Will you be coming again Tessa?' she asked a little anxiously.

'I'm not sure,' Tessa murmured. And then, seeing Melanie's face cloud over, and not wanting to be unkind, for Melanie seemed quite nice really, she went on, 'It isn't really my sort of thing, Melanie.'

'We're all going to church tomorrow and we meet outside at 10.15,' went on the other girl quickly, as though she hadn't spoken, 'and it's not at all boring, and we sing choruses and . . . and . . . I'm sure you'd like it,' she said eagerly.

'No, I don't think I'll be coming,' Tessa said again, and tried not to notice the disappointment in Melanie's eyes.

Then the twins were bounding up to them, and Tessa was glad of the interruption. But not for long, for Peter – his snub nose a mass of freckles and his skin beginning to peel – burst out, 'Hi Tess, we've had a smashing time, and do you know what! Paula and I are going to a 'squash' this evening, and tomorrow we're going to church!'

Tessa, who had no idea what a squash was, and certainly didn't care, looked quickly at Paula, waiting for her to deny such treason. But Paula's face, also red and freckled, wore a beaming smile as she said, 'Yes we are, Tessa. Are you coming?'

Tessa was aware of Melanie close by, and of the twins' unblinking stares. And to make matters worse, one or two of the others had heard snatches of the conversation. In fact, it seemed to her that everyone was standing around waiting for her to answer.

'No, I'm not,' she muttered, glaring at the twins, and not caring very much whether or not anybody heard. Peter and Paula looked a bit crestfallen at Tessa's refusal, but next minute they were scampering away up the steps, feeling guilty, Tessa hoped, for having let her down and deserted her. She felt like calling out 'Turncoats!' after them, but of course she couldn't. At the top of the cliff she caught up with them, and grabbing each by the shoulder, marched them off in the direction of home.

3: Danger!

It was the following Tuesday, and ever since Sunday morning Tessa had been feeling rather lonely and out of it, though she wouldn't have admitted it.

The twins had gone off promptly at 10.15 to St Cuthbert's, which was very small and old and stood outside the village up a winding country lane with high hedges, right on the cliff top. Like the Coastguard Cottages, it was exposed to all winds and weathers, and ever since she had first seen it last week, she had tried to imagine what it would be like to walk between the grave stones up the path to the little porch, on a dark winter's night, with the wind blowing a gale.

In her heart of hearts, she had been sorry not to be going with the twins, for she would have liked to see inside the church, which Uncle had said was Saxon. Ancient churches fascinated her, with their funny fusty smell and beautiful stained glass windows; she liked to wander about outside amongst the leaning tombstones and read the names and ages of the people who were buried beneath the big stone slabs. The more she thought about last Sunday, the more disappointed she felt — just as though she had missed out on something, and she made up her mind that she would visit St Cuthbert's on her own one day, when there wasn't anybody about.

The twins had come back from church with cheerful, smiling faces, full of the service they had been to — though Tessa couldn't understand what there was to get so excited about. Yet she had to admit that they had been less quarrelsome and argumentative since they had come back from the 'squash' the evening before. Paula had even put on a clean cotton frock for the occasion, instead of her grubby jeans and t-shirt which she wore every day. And Peter had looked neat and smart in a pair of green shorts and a crisp white shirt instead of his usual scruffy gear. Paula had brushed her auburn hair until it shone and tied it back with two green bows, instead of having it hanging untidily around her face, whilst Peter's face and hands were remarkably clean, which was certainly unusual.

They had kept singing funny little hymns too, which they called 'choruses', and there was one in particular about a foolish man who built his house on the sand, and a wise one who built his on a rock – which stuck in her mind, for it had a catchy tune, and there were actions to go with it, which the twins had performed with great gusto, so that she had had to smile at their enthusiasm.

The following morning they had gone off to Poltuan Beach promptly at 10.30 to 'help dig the pulpit' as they said, their swimming gear tucked firmly under their arms, *and* carrying surf-boards, which made her feel even more regretful. In the afternoon they had disappeared with the 'beach mission lot' again for a walk along the cliffs, and she was left on her own and didn't see them until they returned in the evening. She had felt a little bit envious, but she still had no intention of going with them.

Auntie seemed worried that Tessa was being left so much on her own all of a sudden and had taken her down to Trewinth Cove in the afternoon – which she had quite enjoyed, until Auntie started telling her that she ought to go along with the twins and enjoy herself.

'You'd like it dear, I'm sure,' she had said, but Tessa had just shrugged and gone on reading her book.

Eventually, on Tuesday, after they had all had an early

lunch so the twins could be off again by two Tessa told Auntie that she intended to walk a little way along the cliffs, assuring her that she wouldn't go far. So she set off in the direction of Trewinth, but when she got to Poltuan Beach she just couldn't resist it, and ran down the steps to the cove. The beach was bathed in sunshine and it looked so lovely that she almost forgot her disappointment about not going to Switzerland.

There were a lot of people around sunbathing, and she sat on a rock for a while watching the sun sparkling on the water and the bathers floating on their polystyrene boards, for the sea was very calm. Catching sight of a dog chasing a ball, she was reminded of Sheba and she wondered how the spaniel was getting on. It occurred to her then that if she had gone along with the twins, she might have met David Jenkins again and he would have told her. In fact, he might even have suggested her going home with him to see her. And now she wouldn't have the chance!

That made her feel a bit miserable, so she looked at the rugged coastline sweeping far to east and west and the gulls squawking on the rocks. Then she remembered Melanie, who she had quite liked and who had clearly been disappointed that she didn't intend to come again. And all the others too, who had really been quite nice and friendly. She'd even liked Sally and Steve until they had been cross with her for swimming out so far, and she pulled a face at the thought, for looking back on it, it did seem rather a silly thing to do, especially after Uncle and Auntie had warned her of the dangers. But there hadn't been any flag flying, for this little beach wasn't dangerous like the other one.

She picked up a handful of sand and let it run through her fingers; and as she did so the chorus the twins had been singing about the man who built his house on the sand came into her mind, and she thought it rather a stupid thing to do. Then, tired of thinking, she looked at the sea again and the rocks which ran out to the right of the cove. Suddenly she caught her breath with excitement, for an idea had come into her head which made her heart beat rather fast, and without stopping to think, she jumped up and ran over the damp, oozing sand, dangling her sandals in her hand by their straps.

No one took any notice of her as she reached the jutting cliff for they were all too busy enjoying themselves, so she stood and looked at the granite headland for a moment before paddling into the water.

The rocks were covered with seaweed and felt very slippery as she started clambering over them, and once or twice she lost her footing and nearly fell into the sea, cutting her foot badly on one that was particularly jagged. But she was almost round the corner, so she kept going even though she was feeling very scared because all she could see was the rugged cliff to her right, and the sea swirling round her, quite deep in parts, on the other side.

Then she was there, and she jumped off a high rock onto the wet sand and drew in her breath with delight. It was like a real desert island beach that faced her; not a human being in sight – only the seabirds running along in little groups at the edge of the water.

She set off slowly along the shoreline, splashing in the shallow water and enjoying being free and all alone. She started to walk over the smooth, untrodden shore in the direction of the tall, sheer cliffs which towered far above her head and made her feel very small and unimportant, and there, a little way in front of her, was the cave!

All her niggling worries were forgotten as she stood and looked at it, and the next minute she was moving eagerly towards it. But as she drew nearer, she saw that it was vast and black and a little bit frightening too. So she took a deep breath and stepped inside, looking all round and feeling the sand cold and damp under her feet. Staring up at the wet, slimy walls rising far above her head she could hear, from somewhere not very far away, a steady plop, plop of water.

She went further into the cave and shivered, feeling suddenly cold and clammy; and a blob of water fell onto her head from the roof and dripped down her neck. Her courage deserted her then and she turned and ran back to the entrance and out onto the beach, relieved to feel the sunshine warming her once more and the sand burning the soles of her feet. But why, she wondered, had she been so scared?

As there didn't seem to be any path up the cliff, she walked slowly on until she reached the other end of the beach where the rocks ran out into the sea again and divided this beach from yet another one. There was quite a wide stretch of sand and it looked inviting, so she hesitated only a minute before going on. But as she walked further round the corner it became much rockier, until before her stretched a long, grey shore, boulder-strewn and a bit sinister.

She supposed she ought to go back and remembered guiltily that she had told Auntie she wouldn't be long. But curiosity drove her on, and she started jumping from rock to rock, nimbler now and careful to avoid the brown bladder-wrack and green seaweed which was everywhere. Presently she reached a big empty gulley which ran from the water's edge right the way up the beach to the foot of the cliff.

She stopped again, something telling her to go no further. But suddenly she was climbing down into the gulley and scrambling out up the other side. Just above the gulley she noticed another cave, much bigger than the one she had been into before, and started walking towards it. She paused in the entrance, and took a few steps forward. Suddenly she stiffened and stood perfectly still, for she could hear voices! Startled, for she certainly hadn't expected there to be anyone here but herself – the beach had no way down to it from the cliff-top – she stared into the dimness of the cave, and at that moment two men appeared out of the blackness, dressed in faded blue denim trousers and t-shirts. They didn't see her at first because they were looking behind them and talking rapidly to each other, but she smiled politely at them when they turned round, because it seemed the right thing to do.

To her surprise they didn't smile back or say 'Good afternoon', but just stared at her and looked a bit taken aback, as though they didn't think she ought to have been there. Which probably she shouldn't have, come to think of it, but it made her feel like an intruder, which was silly really for she certainly had as much right to the beach as they had, she told herself.

Then to her dismay, the taller of the two men had grabbed her by the shoulder and was frowning down at her.

'You'd better not go in there, kid,' he said in a rough sort of voice. 'It's dangerous.'

'You might get hit by a falling boulder,' added the second man quickly.

Alarmed, Tessa turned and walked back to the entrance with them, and then with a quick glance at each other, the men left her.

It was kind of them to have warned her, she supposed, as she watched them walk off over the rocks. Then she went slowly the other way, but she could still feel the pressure of the man's fingers on her shoulder. Glancing back, she saw them leaping from boulder to boulder; but she soon forgot all about them, and glad to be out in the sunshine again, she sat down on a flat rock and stared into the clear, limpid depths of a rockpool.

There were lots of little shrimps which were almost transparent, darting about in it, and a small fish with a blunt head lurked amongst the fronds of seaweed, her shadow on the water making it afraid. Now and again a crab would come out from some hidden recess, and scuttle rapidly over the bed of the pool, looking for shelter again under a stone and pretty pink anemones waved their tiny tentacles. It really was a most interesting pool, and she wished she had got a piece of string and some bait.

She must have sat there on that hard rock, completely absorbed, for quite some time. For she suddenly became aware that the atmosphere had grown strangely cool and that a stiff breeze had sprung up. The sun too, had disappeared behind a big, threatening bank of cloud right overhead, and the sea behind her sounded a bit choppy.

She looked round quickly and to her alarm, instead of a flat, calm ocean, she saw a stretch of sullen grey water tossing itself into angry little peaks, with a thick mist swirling above it, blotting everything out. Worse still, she could hear the cold slap of waves on the rocks quite close to her, and the swishing of water almost at her feet.

Thoroughly alarmed by now, she sprang to her feet and stared down into the gulley. To her amazement and dismay, she saw that it was rapidly filling up with water, the sea swirling into it at such a rate that it was already quite deep all the way up to the foot of the cliff. Terror gripped her as she stood on top of the rock looking down into the gulley, and she bitterly regretted that she had been so stupid as not to notice what had been going on around her.

The first drops of rain spattered down on her and the mist hung round her in wreaths; panic-stricken, she took to her heels and started jumping from rock to rock, making for the far end of the beach.

She hadn't gone very far, though, when to her surprise and delight, she saw the two men again, coming out of another cave just ahead; she gave a great shuddering sigh of relief, for she had forgotten all about them. Where they had been all the time, she couldn't imagine—exploring the caves, she supposed, although they had warned *her* against doing so. She didn't care about that though, and she started shouting at the top of her voice, 'Wait for me! Please wait for me!'

They must have heard her, she was sure, for they were quite close really. Yet they took no notice and didn't even look round. Instead they too started leaping over the rocks, whilst she stumbled after them, hair streaming out behind, not caring that they didn't seem to want to have anything to do with her — only anxious to catch up with them so that she wouldn't be left alone in this terrible place.

Yet it soon became clear to Tessa that they had no intention of stopping. And being a lot bigger and taller, they were covering the ground at much greater speed than she could. Desperate now, she struggled on, but very soon the distance between them widened, and before long she saw them reach the far end of the beach where the rocks jutted out and the spray rose high as the waves pounded against them.

Why, oh why, she thought again, her mouth dry and her breath coming in great gasps, hadn't she taken Uncle's and Auntie's warnings seriously? She ran on, slipping and slithering time and time again and all the time she was calling out, 'Wait! Please wait!', unable to believe that the men could be so cruel as to leave her to her fate. But by now they had reached the headland and were climbing higher and higher over the huge, jagged rocks, just out of reach of the angry sea. Until at last they disappeared from her terrified gaze, around the corner into the next bay, and she was alone.

Sick with fear, she reached the spot where they had started to climb, but she knew it was too late, and that the gigantic waves would sweep her from the rocks if she tried to follow them.

So she stood quite still, watching the sea surging into a big pool at her feet, the water growing deeper with every second, and it seemed to her at that moment that this must be some horrible nightmare from which she would awake!

Yet it was no nightmare, but stark reality, and she turned and ran blindly back towards the gulley. But when she reached it, it was awash with water right up to the very top, as she had known it would be, and escape that way was impossible too.

She was cut off by the tide with a fine drizzle falling and a chilly wind blowing in from the sea, whipping it into great breakers. The mist swirled all round her, freezing her to the bone, and terrified out of her wits, she stared up at the face of the cliff, but there was no escape there either. For it towered above her, unclimbable and menacing.

And then – almost for the first time in her life – she prayed. And almost immediately a strange thing happened.

4: A Miracle

It seemed to Tessa that she could hear a tune that was somehow familiar! At first, in her dazed state, she thought it was running through her own head, but she couldn't put any words to it, no matter how hard she tried. It seemed to come and go, getting louder and then dying away. And now and again – for a minute or two – the wind would snatch it away from her altogether, so that she couldn't even hear it.

She held her breath, straining her ears, and staring up towards the cliff-top – for it was from there, she guessed, that the sound was coming. But she could see nothing, for the mist floated before her eyes, blotting out the landscape. Her t-shirt was sodden and her jeans clung damply to her legs as she stood there, so that her teeth chattered and she shivered with cold and fright.

Then suddenly she remembered! It was one of those choruses that the twins had been singing over and over again ever since last Saturday evening when they had come back from the 'squash'. But what were the words? She tried hard to remember, for somehow it seemed terribly important that she should. Then suddenly they came to her so clearly that she thought for one moment that the twins were standing at her elbow singing them, and that she was back at home with Auntie and Uncle.

> *Jesus is with me,*
> *With me all day . . .*

Then her mind went quite blank and she couldn't think what came next . . . though she could remember how the chorus finished – or almost.

> *With me at home*
> *And wherever I go,*
> *How I should love him . . .*

and she screwed up her eyes tightly, trying to think of the last line and suddenly it came to her.

> *Who watches me so.*

Watching her? Was Jesus really watching her, there on this grey, cold shore with the waves thundering up behind her, and the cliffs in front, tall and impossible to climb. And if He was, did He care about her plight? Was He really with her? Oh, how she wished she knew!

It certainly didn't seem like it for there was no way of escape that she knew of, and why, oh why hadn't she gone along with the twins to the beach services, for then perhaps she would have found out the answers to her questions. Had she done so, she would have been treasure-hunting with them and safe at home now, instead of here in this terrible plight.

Another chorus flashed into her mind – something about prayer changing things. She wasn't sure if it did – she had never really thought about it before – but now she was desperate, and for the first time in her life she found herself telling God that she had been very silly – just like the man who built his house upon the sand – and that she needed His help – badly.

And the next moment it seemed to her that a miracle had happened, for she knew that someone actually *was* singing – or rather whistling – on the cliff-top just above her head. It hadn't been her imagination, after all!

'Help!' she called, standing on a flat rock, wet and bedraggled, and with the mist swirling all round her and the rain falling in a thin, damping drizzle. 'Help!' she called again. And above the tearing gale and the thundering waves, her voice rose shrill with terror, only to die away the next minute on a choking sob. For it seemed to her as she strained her ears to listen, that whoever it was who had been up there on top of the cliff had gone away without taking any notice. For the whistling had quite stopped, and the thought came to her that perhaps it had been those two men up there – the ones who had gone away and left her there, and didn't want to know.

So she called out 'Help!' once more with all the strength she could muster, and suddenly a voice called back 'Hello there!' and someone was looking down at her from the very edge of the cliff – someone she had seen before somewhere, but with the swirling greyness between her and whoever it was, she couldn't think where. Until she saw the dog, and then she knew!

Sheba! It was Sheba – and her young master must be up there with her. And she gave a big shuddering sigh of relief for the second time that afternoon, and blinked back the tears which ran in salty rivulets down her wet face, mingling with the rain. For this time help was surely at hand!

Or was it? For what could David Jenkins – a boy of fourteen and not much older than herself – do to help? But of course David's father was the coastguard, wasn't he? And it was the job of coastguards to rescue people in difficulties, she remembered. So what better person could God have sent along to help her?

'Don't worry Tessa! I – I'll think of something . . .'

The look of surprise and alarm on David's face had given way to one of concentration as he peered down at her from way above her head. A moment later he started speaking again – calmly and slowly – as he wriggled even closer to the edge of the cliff.

'I want you to climb up to that little green tussock just above where you're standing ... Can you Tessa ...? There's a little ledge up there where you can sit ...'

The rest of what he was saying Tessa couldn't hear, for a gust of wind whipped it away. But she knew which tussock he meant and, wide awake now, she ran towards the base of the cliff and started to climb, though her legs were trembling so much she thought they would give way. It wasn't as difficult as she had expected though, once she got going, and finding a foothold here and there, she made progress – slow but sure – encouraged by the voice which came to her faintly from above.

'That's right, Tessa ... just over to your left. You'll be safe there and out of reach of the sea, I think ...'

Her head was level with the tussock now, and sure enough there was the little ledge, just big enough for her to sit on, though she hadn't noticed it from down on the beach. She made a great effort and hauled herself up onto it, gripping the edge with her hands so that she wouldn't slip off. She was so relieved to be out of reach of that boiling mass of ocean – even though she was shivering and chilled through and through – that she started to sob again and this time she just let the tears trickle down her face without even trying to stop them. Even the fact that the ledge was very narrow and she knew that if she didn't hold on tightly she might go sliding down the cliff again, didn't bother her too much now. For help was at hand.

From where she was sitting she couldn't see David, for she dared not turn her head to look up. But his voice came down to her again in a short while, calm and reassuring.

'I want you to sit there until I come back, Tessa. Try not to worry. You'll be quite safe now ... I ...'

She strained her ears to hear as his voice became fainter and fainter in the gale which was rising. But the rest of it was completely lost, except that she thought she caught the words 'motor-boat'. Then it came to her again more clearly as he shouted: 'I'll pick you up . . . won't be long . . . Keep your pecker up . . .'

She called up, 'All right,' in a small voice which the wind blew mockingly back at her. Now that some of the danger seemed past, her terror and panic were beginning to give way to other feelings of a different sort, and she started to feel guilty and ashamed. For how could she have been so silly and thoughtless as to forget the other warnings Auntie and Uncle had given her about making sure she didn't go wandering on lonely beaches, and always to be certain she knew whether the tide was going out or coming in? These had been the first things they had warned her and the twins about when they had arrived, she remembered.

Left on her own again, panic came back as she gazed horrified at the sea hissing and churning amongst the rocks only a few feet below. And she gasped when she saw that the rock on which she had been standing only twenty minutes ago was now completely under water. To take her mind off, she started to count the breakers as they tore towards her, noticing confusedly that every seventh wave seemed a lot bigger and more threatening than the rest.

After a while, her brain seemed to become as numb as the rest of her and she couldn't think clearly. Her teeth wouldn't stop chattering either, and her limbs wouldn't stop shaking; she felt so stiff and cramped with sitting in the same position, and her arms ached so much with holding on to the edge of the ledge, that she closed her eyes tightly and wondered vaguely just how much longer she could hang on if help didn't come soon.

Then – just as she had the awful feeling that she was going to faint – there came to her ears above the storm the distant throb of an engine out to sea. Her eyes flew open and – wonder of wonders – there was a motor-boat coming into view around the point. It was making slow progress for the waves were crashing all around it – and sometimes it was lost to view altogether as it sank into the trough of a wave.

But next moment it would rise again, carried high on the crest of another, and she could just make out a lone figure at the helm. She held her breath as she followed the boat's lurching progress, and once it almost turned over altogether, so that she closed her eyes because she couldn't bear to look.

When she opened them for the second time, she saw to her unutterable relief that the little craft was still there. But it seemed to have changed course and for one terrible moment she thought that it was going to turn round and go back again. Then she realised that it was moving in an easterly direction, making for the entrance to the gulley, and she guessed that David was going to try and make a landing that way – which would be a lot safer, of course, than to risk foundering on the rocky shore and getting smashed to pieces.

Eyes glued to the motor-boat and its skipper, she saw that she had been right. Still tossed about like a cockleshell it was entering the gulley, and for a few tense minutes it seemed to be making quite good headway, as it bobbed about on the surging water. Then suddenly a huge wave hit it, and Tessa gave a cry of horror, as it was borne high on the swell and almost disappeared beneath the water. Terrified, she strained her eyes to see, and suddenly it was there again and being carried forward with a rush towards the foot of the cliff.

She gasped and her hand flew to her mouth as the helm of the boat dug itself into the small patch of sand amongst the rocks, and the rear end of the little craft rose high in the air.

But the next second she drew a great breath of relief. For the lone sailor had jumped clear and was reaching for the mooring rope!

5: Rescued

An hour-and-a-half later, Tessa sat huddled in a comfortable armchair in the sitting room at No. 2 Coastguard Cottages in front of the electric fire which had been turned on for her benefit – though outside the sun had broken through the clouds and the mist and rain had cleared away.

She was wrapped up in Mrs Jenkins' cherry-coloured dressing gown, which was much too big for her, but it was warm and that was all that mattered, and there was a blanket around her shoulders as well, because she had heard Mr Jenkins whisper to his wife that she was suffering from shock.

She had stopped shivering now and her fingers and toes were beginning to thaw out as she sipped a mug of steaming chocolate and told the coastguard and his family the sorry tale of her afternoon's adventures. They listened intently, looking rather serious, but they didn't tell her off as she had thought they would, so she supposed they considered she had been punished enough – which she certainly had. They did say how dangerous it could be along that stretch of coast though, and that people much older and wiser than herself had been in the same predicament – which she found comforting somehow.

David, sitting opposite to her and also wrapped in a dressing gown, looked pale underneath his tan, which made her feel even more guilty. For it was all her fault, she knew, and he could have died risking his life to rescue her. She had told him a part of the story already – in disjointed sentences as they walked up the cliff path from the beach below the Coastguard Station, after landing at the jetty there. Fortunately the tide had just turned and the storm had begun to blow itself out by the time she had helped David to launch the motor-boat. So though the sea had been still very choppy, it hadn't been so dangerous going back. All the same, she had been very frightened as the little boat tossed about like a cork, and David strained every muscle to keep it on course.

When she reached the part about the two men leaving her behind on the beach, thinking only of saving their own skins, she saw David glance quickly at his parents, after which Mr Jenkins asked her in a quiet voice if she could remember what they looked like and how old they were – only he said it quite casually as though it wasn't of very much importance to him to know the answers. Which, of course, made Tessa wonder if it was, but she couldn't seem to fix her thoughts on anything for more than two seconds at a time just at the moment. So she tried to picture the two men again.

'One was quite tall,' she said at last. 'About . . . about six foot, I should think, with darkish hair – rather long. And the other was a bit shorter and fatter, with light coloured hair.'

She wasn't very good at guessing people's ages, but she said she thought they looked around twenty-five, and she remembered that they were both wearing blue denims and sweat shirts.

'Perhaps they didn't hear you calling out to them,' Mrs Jenkins suggested, and Tessa said thoughtfully, 'No, perhaps they didn't,' and remembered that they had been kind in warning her about the caves, but it was all very confusing and her head ached.

Then Mr Jenkins was explaining that they had kept her

here rather than running her straight home in the car, because for one thing it was nearer – and they had also thought it might be a bit of a shock for her Aunt and Uncle to see her arrive home looking like a drowned rat without any warning. He had, of course, telephoned them immediately David and she had arrived back, glossing over the more alarming details of what had happened, so that they wouldn't be too worried. He would run Tessa back just as soon as she had recovered a little, he had told them, and in the meantime they were not to worry, for she was in good hands.

Tessa learnt too that after she had set off for her walk after lunch, her Aunt had gone into the garden to do some weeding, and when the rain had started around three-thirty, she had expected Tessa to walk in at any minute. The twins had come back soon afterwards – earlier than usual because the treasure-hunt had had to be abandoned – and when Tessa didn't turn up, she had been very worried, and putting on her mac had set off in the direction of Trewinth to look for her.

Of course her Aunt had never thought of looking over the cliff where those deserted beaches lay, and when there was no sign of Tessa, she had got really anxious and had returned home soaked through to ring Uncle at his office. Uncle had arrived back as soon as he could get away, and they had been about to set out to look for Tessa together, when Mr Jenkins had rung with the good news that she was found.

What a lot of worry and trouble she had caused everybody, Tessa thought miserably, as she nibbled at a biscuit and listened to what David was telling her about how he came to be on the cliff-top just at the right moment.

He had set out with the treasure-hunting party immediately after lunch, he said, and they had been having great fun until the rain came down and spoilt it all. Arriving home, he had gone straight out again with Sheba who, since her accident, hadn't been allowed to go for walks by herself because her injured leg hadn't quite healed – though fortunately it had turned out to be nothing worse than a bad sprain.

Tessa knew what had happened after that, of course, and now – looking at the spaniel stretched out at her feet – she felt a little bit happier, for it was lovely to see her again when she hadn't expected to do so.

As to the actual rescue operation, although she knew only too well about the last part of it, she wasn't told about the first bit until a long time afterwards. After he had left her sitting on the ledge, David had arrived home breathless from running, hoping his father might be in. But he wasn't and neither was his mother, so in order not to waste a lot of valuable time fetching help, he had decided to set out alone in the motor-boat, which Tessa learned was really just an ordinary rowing-boat with an outboard motor. Launching the little boat from the jetty in the cove beneath the coastguard station had been a perilous operation, and the tiny craft had come very near to getting broken up on the rugged shoreline even before it rounded the point. It had only been David's skill and bravery that had prevented it from capsizing, and the presence of mind with which he had changed course and steered for the gulley had saved both their lives.

David had been 'messing about in boats' ever since he was a toddler, his parents told Tessa, but judging by the looks of pride they kept giving their son as he sat by the fire sipping his hot drink, she realised that they must both be feeling very proud of him.

After she had slept for a while, Tessa awoke feeling a little brighter and was able to change back into her clothes which Mrs Jenkins had been busy drying out for her. Before leaving, she thanked David again rather shyly, and Mrs

Jenkins kissed her and told her not to worry any more. Then Mr Jenkins went to bring the car round to the front door and Tessa got in and they were off, though the nearer they got to the bungalow, the worse she felt, for she was dreading meeting Uncle and Auntie.

She needn't have worried though, for as soon as they got there, she saw Uncle and Auntie standing at the gate, and they were looking so relieved to see her back safe and sound that she guessed they – like the Jenkins – must have thought she had been punished enough. After thanking the coastguard warmly, they invited him in for a cup of tea, and he stayed awhile and chatted about other things. Then he said goodbye, and when he had gone, Auntie told Tessa it would be a good idea if she had an early night.

She wasn't sorry to get into bed, but after Auntie had given her a goodnight kiss, she did extract a promise from her, that she wouldn't wander off on her own any more, and Tessa was only too willing to give it, for of course she had had a terrible fright.

Besides which, before she left the Coastguard Cottage, David had also got her to promise something, which was that she would come to the beach service the next morning – and somewhat to her surprise, she had found herself eagerly agreeing. If she could be there early, he told her – around a quarter to ten – he would look out for her and she could help to decorate the pulpit if she liked. She wasn't sure what that involved, but it sounded interesting and she even found herself looking forward to the next day.

As for the twins, as soon as they heard of her escapade when they came back from playing with their friends at the house next door but one, they seemed to look upon their elder sister as some sort of hero. She knew she was really just the reverse – but she suspected that they rather wished it had happened to them instead of to her so that they could have boasted about it to their friends! Though they weren't told the whole story by any means!

Sleep was a long time coming to Tessa and she lay awake until nearly midnight, tossing and turning and staring up at the ceiling as she re-lived the terror of all she had been through.

Then the words of the chorus that David had been whistling on the top of the cliff ran through her head again, and she remembered to say 'thank you' to God for getting her out of such a terrible mess.

She felt calmer after that, but just before she dozed off, the two men who had been on the beach with her came into her mind, though she had been trying not to think about *them*. She had horrible nightmares in which she dreamed that instead of her chasing after them, it was the other way round and they were running after her, and her legs felt as heavy as lead so that she couldn't get away from them.

It was a great relief to wake up next morning and see the sunshine pouring in through her bedroom window, with Auntie bringing her a cup of tea, and everything back to normal again.

At least she thought it was!

6: God's Mighty Army

Tessa and the twins left for Poltuan promptly at 9.45 the next morning, and if Peter and Paula were surprised to have Tessa's company, they didn't show it, but chattered non-stop as they skipped along the narrow country lanes.

The tide was going out and the sun already quite hot by the time they arrived, and groups of holiday-makers with picnic baskets and all the other equipment necessary for a day by the sea, were trekking across the cliffs from the camp site, or climbing down the steep narrow pathway to the big sandy beach.

Tessa and the twins went by way of the sand-dunes which was the quickest route for them, and as soon as they came over the top, they spotted the little group of children and adults gathered by the rocks on the far side of the huge sandy bay. They could see the big red banner too, with the words 'BEACH MISSION' on it in large white capital letters, which was being anchored with ropes by Steve and two or three other adults; and the twins, eager to be there, broke into a run, leaving Tessa to follow more slowly.

As she got nearer, she could see that the 'pulpit' was taking shape too, as boys and girls shovelled sand on to it with spades – though it wasn't the same as a real pulpit, but more like a long platform in the sand. By the time she got there, she was feeling rather shy and self-conscious, but almost at once Steve was coming towards her, seeming pleased to see her.

'Hello Tessa,' he said. 'So glad you've come!' and then

Sally too walked over to speak to her – just as though the little incident on the beach last Saturday afternoon when she had swum out too far had been quite forgotten. But she did find herself wondering whether they had heard about her latest escapade, though she certainly hoped they hadn't!

'Hi Tessa! Glad you made it!' said someone else. And it was David this time, with a spade in his hand. 'We're just going to put the text on the front of the pulpit,' he went on, 'and what we do is to draw the letters in the sand with sticks, then pick them out with pebbles and seaweed. The one for today is "GOD SO LOVED THE WORLD".'

Melanie bounced up to them at that moment, all smiles, and told Tessa that she could either help with drawing in the letters, or collect the pebbles and shells and things – whichever she liked, and Tessa, to whom it all felt very new and strange, said she would do the same as Melanie.

So the two girls went off together with a pail each, and were soon back with them filled to the brim with pretty shells and unusual looking pebbles, for they would need quite a lot, Melanie told her. Tessa looked towards the pulpit and saw that David and the others had just finished doing the lettering, and Melanie said she would show her how to fill in the letters. She soon got the hang of it, and with several other boys and girls helping, it didn't take very long and was quite fun really. When at last they reached the full-stop at the end of the sentence, Tessa straightened up and stood back to see the effect of what they had done.

The text looked really rather nice, she thought, and it was big enough and clear enough to be seen almost on the other side of the beach. Yet as she looked at it, the words didn't mean very much to her, for though she and the twins had been sent to Sunday School by their parents when she was very young, the habit had been dropped as she grew older, and Sunday was a day when they were taken out to the sea or into the countryside all day.

Soon lots more children began to arrive, so that by twenty-five past ten there were about fifty of them gathered around the pulpit. Tessa sat near the back, in between Melanie and David, and from there she could see Peter and Paula in the front row with their friends. She was aware too of people sitting in deck-chairs or lying around on the sand sunbathing, not far away, and she noticed that some of them stared curiously in their direction, though most of them, after the first casual glance, didn't take any more notice.

Promptly at ten-thirty, one of the adults whom she didn't know, but who Melanie said was called Barry, sprinted onto the pulpit without bothering to use the steps dug into the back of it, and gave everyone a warm welcome. After that he gave out the first hymn which was *All Things Bright and Beautiful*, which Tessa knew of course, though she hadn't sung it for a very long time. She enjoyed singing it now with all the others – for everything did seem very beautiful – the cloudless blue sky, the sun dancing on the water, the tossing waves and the vast stretch of golden sand – though she shuddered a little as she looked at the cliffs, remembering the previous afternoon.

Barry got down from the pulpit and Sally took his place, and Tessa saw that she had a Bible in her hand. She opened it and said that the reading was to be taken from Chapter 3 of the Gospel according to St John – the one from which the text on the pulpit had been taken, which was verse 16, and even Tessa knew that reference. Then they were singing choruses from the sheets that had been handed round, and being asked to choose their favourites.

The twins called out one that was fast becoming very familiar to Tessa – the one about the wise man and the foolish man, and they all sang it with great enthusiasm, putting in the actions which most of them knew, but which Sally went through with them first, for the benefit of the newcomers. Next someone was asking for another chorus which was similar, but quite new to her, and which went:

> *Build on the rock*
> *The rock which ever stands,*
> *Build on the rock,*
> *And not upon the sand.*
> *You need not fear the storm*
> *Or the earthquake shock,*
> *You're safe for evermore*
> *If you build on the rock.*

It had a nice tune, and everyone clapped loudly on the words 'shock' and 'rock' at the end. Both choruses seemed to fit in very well, considering where they were, thought Tessa, though she wasn't quite certain *what* rock they kept singing about. She looked at a limpet-covered one to her right, but she was sure it didn't mean that one, or any of the others which lay all around them. Yet it did seem as though that last chorus might have been chosen specially with her in mind because of the bit about the storm.

Then the notices were given out, with details of the programme for the next few days, which included another 'squash' – whatever that might mean – a treasure-hunt, and a walk over Bodmin Moor the next Saturday afternoon, to be followed by a barbecue at a nearby cove in the evening, all of which sounded rather exciting.

After that they sang some more choruses and the time went very quickly. Looking round, Tessa noticed that quite a lot of people who had been sitting at a distance had moved a little nearer so as to hear what was going on, and several children building sandcastles had left their buckets and spades and were hovering on the outskirts of the group.

Steve got up to speak next, and opened his Bible at the chapter which had just been read to them – the one about Nicodemus coming to Jesus by night. He put the story into very simple language, so that even the youngest there could understand, explaining that being a Christian wasn't a question of trying to be kind and helpful to other people and doing one's best at school – though of course these things were very important. For the trouble was, he said, that no matter how hard one tried, or how good one might be, one couldn't ever hope to measure up to God's standard, because it was too high for even the very best.

He went on to explain that what one had to do was to have faith, or to believe, as the text went on to say, on God's Son, the Lord Jesus Christ. That meant acknowledging that He was God's son, and that God had sent Him into the world to die for men and women, boys and girls everywhere, on the cross at Calvary nearly two thousand years ago.

The next step was to confess that we were sinners needing a Saviour, ask Jesus to come into our hearts and forgive us our sins, and then – if we really meant it – He would cleanse us and give us the gift of everlasting life, so that when we died we would go to live with Him in Heaven for ever and ever.

And when we had done that, he explained, we would be like the wise man in the chorus, who built his house on the rock. But if we didn't, then we would be like the other man – the foolish one – who built his house on the sand, without any foundation to enable it to stand up against the storm.

'So *that* was what it meant!' Tessa thought eagerly.

Steve said next that, having asked Jesus Christ into our lives, the devil would be very busy trying to distract us and make us turn away from following Him, but by reading our Bibles every day and by prayer, we would learn what God wanted us to do with our lives, and so be kept close to Him.

Tessa sat spellbound, for it was all new to her – at least a lot of it was, for she had never heard it put so clearly before –

and when Steve prayed a short prayer and asked them to repeat it silently in their hearts after him, if they really meant it—she did, telling Jesus that she was a sinner, that she believed in Him, and wanted Him to come into her heart.

At the end, they stood to sing the final hymn which was *Onward Christian Soldiers*—a lovely rousing one—and she felt very glad, as she sang it with the others, that she now belonged to God's mighty army, along with David, the twins, Melanie, Steve, Sally and a lot of the others.

After the closing prayer, she helped to pack up the hymn books and chorus sheets, and when there was a chance to speak to Steve, she asked him for one of the little booklets which he had told them would be helpful.

Then she went off for a surf-bathe with everyone else, and looking back on that day afterwards, she felt that it would be something she would remember for the whole of her life, for everything seemed absolutely marvellous suddenly—or almost everything.

For there was a little niggling worry at the back of her mind that perhaps this was all too good to last, and a sort of foreboding which she could not shake off, but she was soon changing into her swimsuit and someone lent her a surfboard.

So she ran down to the sea with Melanie and the others, and jumped over the waves as she saw everyone else doing, and it didn't take long to get wet because before you knew where you were, they had broken all over you. David and Melanie showed her how to use the surf-board and she soon forgot all her troubles again, for it was as much fun as she had expected, if not more.

There seemed to be hundreds of surfers all around them, they were coming from all directions, the breakers were absolutely enormous further out, so that she was a bit scared at first. But there was no need to go very far out, she soon found, for the smaller waves had plenty of power behind them and, after a little practice, she was able to judge exactly the right moment to get down on her board, so that she would be carried swiftly up the beach in a flurry of spray!

It was great and terribly exciting – and when at last they all came out, it was a scramble to get dressed and back in time for lunch.

7: Who are the two men?

The weather went on being hot and sunny and with the beach services, the surf bathing, and the activities arranged for the afternoons, the next two days seemed to Tessa the happiest she had ever spent.

On Thursday evening, she and the twins went on a fishing trip with Uncle, and they were lucky enough to catch seven mackerel which they carried proudly home, tied together with a piece of string. Auntie cooked them for their supper – they tasted lovely with lemon squeezed all over them, and they were promised a lobster supper before long.

On Friday afternoon there was another treasure hunt, to make up for the one that had been rained off last Tuesday, and they all wandered over the cliffs looking for the clues which had been carefully hidden by Steve and Barry.

To Tessa's great delight, David had brought Sheba along too, and she was glad to see that the spaniel's leg seemed better again, so that she was able to chase around looking for rabbits. Sheba hadn't forgotten Tessa either, for as soon as she saw her, she made a bee-line for her, leaping up to cover her face with wet kisses.

'That's her way of saying "Thank you",' David laughed, and Tessa was so pleased to see her that she almost forgot they were supposed to be looking for treasure, until Melanie said they had better get a move on as the others were almost out of sight. They found a few of the clues, but had to give up in the end when it was announced that the 'treasure' – a box of chocolates – had been tracked down to a cleft in a rock on the beach.

Saturday came, and Tessa could hardly believe that only a week had gone by since she and the twins had found Sheba on the cliff. Such a lot had happened in that time that it seemed much longer in one way. Though at the same time, the days seemed to have absolutely flown.

In the afternoon they all piled into the coach with their picnic teas, and set off for Bodmin Moor. Tessa and the twins had only seen the moor from the train so far – on their way down from London ten days ago – and Tessa had thought it flat and uninteresting then.

Yet now, sitting next to Melanie as they travelled along the narrow, winding lanes, she found herself looking eagerly out of the windows at the fields of cattle and sheep. The tall hedges looked so pretty – full of lacy cow parsley and honeysuckle – and she was beginning to like Cornwall more every day because it was different from anywhere she had ever been.

She felt different herself too, since last Wednesday when she had become a Christian – though now and then she didn't. Like last night, for instance, when she had got annoyed with the twins for talking when she was trying to read, and this morning when she had grumbled a bit about having to lay the table for breakfast when Auntie asked her to.

She sighed now as she thought about it, and then Melanie was laughing, and pointing out the funny names on the signposts which they passed, most of which, as they had already discovered, began with either Tre, Pol or Pen.

They turned into a lane and there before them was the moor, flat and rather mysterious, stretching away into the distance, and their coach driver pointed out the two highest points which were called Brown Willy and Rough Tor – pronounced 'Rowter' by the locals, he said. They were to stop at Rough Tor and anyone who wished to do so could climb the mountain.

Everyone was keen to, and they set off laughing and talking, determined to reach the top. Nearly all of them got there, though it was quite a long haul. But it was worth it just to see the moor stretching away on all sides, with Brown Willy not far away. Then it was time to come down again and get back into the coach, for their next stop was to be Dozmary Pool.

They had been told that the pool was a rather creepy, sinister sort of place, so when they stopped again and caught their first glimpse of it, Tessa felt a bit disappointed. For there before them was a lake – a brilliant patch of blue against the surrounding green, and in the bright sunshine in the middle of the afternoon, it seemed almost the same as any other lake, and not particularly spooky at all. So to cheer her up as they walked across the gorse and heather towards it, David described what it would look like on a cold winter's day, under a grey sky, and with the wind howling all around like a wailing banshee. He made it sound so real that they all shivered and pretended to be scared stiff.

It was a very long narrow pool, and they spread themselves out on the bank at one end to eat their tea. Auntie had given Tessa and the twins a real Cornish pastie each, as well as tasty sandwiches and cakes – just in case they got hungry, and while they ate, David told them some exciting stories about the pool.

One was about a man called Tregeagle who was condemned to work all night and all day for ever, trying to bale the pool dry with a leaky limpet shell – according to another superstition, the pool was bottomless. On hearing this, some of the boys jumped up and started hurling stones towards the middle of it, until David said that this too was only a legend, for at some time during the last century the pool had dried up. Which was rather disappointing, but it made them laugh.

Yet another legend said that there was no life within the waters of the pool – which wasn't true either apparently, for there were plenty of fish in it!

Just then Mike, one of the boys who had been throwing stones, startled everyone with the information that according to the news that morning, two criminals had escaped from Dartmoor ten days ago and were still on the loose. And when he went on to say that they were believed to be on their way down to Cornwall, Melanie whispered to Tessa that she hoped they didn't meet them on the moor! Then David was telling them about someting called the Logan Stone, which was a bit further down on the coast, and though it was very big and you could climb right to the top of it, it was so finely balanced that it was possible to rock it with one finger.

They stayed for a little longer, and just before they left, some cattle with long shaggy coats came down for a drink, standing ankle-deep in the water on the opposite side of the pool. Tessa would have liked to stay there all afternoon, but their next port of call was Jamaica Inn, so about four o'clock they set off back to the coach.

There was another bit of excitement when they reached it, for a short, thickset man with a big black alsatian suddenly appeared. To everybody's alarm, the dog advanced menacingly towards Sheba, growling ferociously – but David managed to grab her collar and clip her lead to it. Then they were off again, travelling on along a long straight road with the moor on either side until they reached a solitary building on the right-hand side, which the coach-driver told them was Jamaica Inn.

So they all looked at it with interest, but Tessa felt a bit disappointed again, for it seemed like any other inn, with lots of holidaymakers about and not a bit creepy. But there again, it would look a lot different on a wild winter's night, as David reminded her.

They tumbled out of the coach and made straight for the big room where refreshments were served, to queue up for ice-cream. The place was quite full, but they managed to find some empty tables and sat chattering for a while, enjoying their Cornish ices, which were lovely and creamy.

Presently David suggested to Tessa and Melanie that they have a wander round. So they got up and followed him out into the passage, and they hadn't walked more than a few yards when Tessa came to a sudden standstill, and clapped her hand to her mouth with a little gasp.

For coming out of the bar at the far end of the passage and going off in the other direction, were two men, and although she could only see their backviews, she knew at once who they were, and all the horror of last Tuesday came surging back to her. David was walking just a yard or two in front of her and Melanie, telling them a creepy tale about the inn in olden days, but she interrupted him, catching hold of his arm, so that he swung round, surprised.

'It's them!' she hissed in a loud whisper. 'Those men!' and a startled look leapt into David's eyes as his head switched round again, and he seemed to know at once what she meant as he followed her horrified gaze. Then the two children stood stockstill, scarcely daring to breathe, with Melanie looking completely bewildered.

Next minute, to Tessa's alarm, David darted forward a few steps before pulling up abruptly. For at that moment there was a diversion, as a boy of about ten came tearing round the corner from the opposite direction, colliding headlong with the two strangers, and rushing on with a muttered 'Sorry!' towards David and the others.

'Can't you look where you're going?' they heard the taller of the two shout after him – the one with the tousled mop of black hair who had gripped Tessa by the shoulder – and they saw him turn and glare at the boy as he sped on down the passage. Then Tessa held her breath for the man's gaze had travelled beyond him to them, and it was too late to look away for he had seen them. As his narrowed eyes focussed on Tessa, a puzzled expression crept into them and it seemed to her that they became suddenly wary as he recognised her. Then he nudged his companion, and the next moment they had turned and were gone, disappearing from view round the corner. Tessa glanced at David again, but she was sure that he was trying to avoid meeting her gaze, though Melanie was staring at her with a worried expression on her face.

'What's the matter, Tessa?' she asked quickly. 'Are you all right?' but Tessa merely murmured that it was nothing much, though Melanie – not to be put off – asked again, 'Who were those men?'

'I can't tell you now,' her friend replied rather impatiently and looked at David again who was still staring up the passage with a thoughtful expression in his eyes. Tessa half expected him to go rushing off in pursuit, but the next moment he shrugged and pulled a wry face. Then he looked towards the girls with a smile that seemed to Tessa a bit forced and not at all like his usual cheery grin.

'Do you know who they are, David?' Tessa whispered so that Melanie couldn't hear, and in imagination she was back in the sitting room of No. 2 Coastguard Cottages again, huddled over the fire drying out, and seeing the look that passed between David and his parents when she had told them about the two men on the beach. At the same time she remembered what Mike had said about the convicts, and she waited eagerly for his reply, but he only shook his head, frowning slightly.

'No Tess, I don't,' he said with a shrug. Then he added casually, 'Pleasant types, from what you tell me!' But she knew he was still thinking about them, and that though he had only caught a fleeting glimpse of them, he had taken note of them and would recognise them again if he saw them.

Why was he so interested in them, she wondered, and why had the incident cast such a cloud over her afternoon?

They looked around for the others then and the spell was broken as they went towards the restaurant where most of the children were still sitting round the tables, completely unaware of the little drama that had just taken place, though Tessa was still shaking. Then Steve and Sally were coming through the door towards them and Steve said, 'Hello there! Enjoying yourselves?' whilst Sally told them that they were just going to have a quick look round before they went. 'Coming with us?' she asked, and David said, 'We might as well,' for all three – though not one of them could take much interest in anything any more, after what had just happened.

Tessa looked at David as they walked along the passage down which the two men had disappeared, and opened her mouth to say something. But he turned away quickly to speak to Steve, and she was sure he didn't want to talk about it any more – though it was probably her imagination, she told herself, as she glanced fearfully around!

There was no sign of the men however, and a quarter-of-an-hour later they joined the rest of the party outside in the courtyard. Everyone climbed into the coach, tired but cheerful, though Tessa and Melanie were still looking subdued as they found their seats.

As soon as they started to move, Melanie whispered again, 'Tessa, who *were* those men?' and Tessa was silent for a moment, trying to think what to say, for there didn't seem any point in worrying Melanie with her stupid fears and suspicions which might be quite unfounded.

So she shrugged and said casually, 'I don't know, Melanie,' which didn't tell her friend very much, but at least it was true. Then she added rather apologetically, for she knew she had sounded a bit abrupt, 'I'll tell you about it some time, Melanie, really I will,' and Melanie didn't say any more, for she must have realised that Tessa was terribly worried and upset.

'We can pray about it, whatever it is anyway, can't we?' Melanie said after a pause, and Tessa said quickly, 'Yes, we can,' and was grateful to her for suggesting it.

Then Tessa almost forgot the whole thing, for their coach-driver took them through a lovely valley thick with fir trees on the sides of the slopes, and there was a river and lots of little houses which looked just like Swiss chalets among the trees. It was so much like the pictures she had seen of Switzerland in fact, that she forgot everything else for the time being, and when they stopped again, some of them got out to take photographs.

Then they were off once more and heading for home, and the two girls started chattering nineteen to the dozen again, just as though nothing had happened, until the coach pulled up in the village street outside the post office.

Sally was standing by the door as they climbed out of the coach, reminding them to be up on the cliff at 7.30 ready to go off to the beach – a different one this time – for the barbecue. Then Tessa found the twins and they set off for home.

But on the way, Tessa suddenly discovered that she hadn't got her purse, which had some money in it, and was a little Welsh tweed one, of which she was rather fond. So telling the twins to go on, she hurried back; Sally was still standing by the door of the coach, but Steve and Barrie were with her, and they were all three talking to David and looking rather serious.

They stopped as soon as they saw her and smiled, asking her if she had enjoyed herself, and had she forgotten something?

So she just said, 'Yes, thank you,' and told them about the purse. Then she ran up the steps to look for it and to her great relief it was lying on the floor near where she had been sitting. So she picked it up and hurried up the road after the twins.

But all her fears had come rushing back, for she was certain she knew what David and the grown-ups had been talking about!

8: Another Fright

The barbecue that evening was a huge success – so much so that it was decided to hold another the next weekend. In the excitement of helping to stoke the bonfire and watching sausages sizzling on the spit, the events of the afternoon got pushed to the back of Tessa's mind.

The next day, Sunday, Tessa put on her favourite green cotton dress, brushed her hair until it shone and with the twins, tucked into eggs and bacon for breakfast, with mushrooms as a special treat.

Then it was time to leave for St Cuthbert's and the three children set off down the little lane opposite the bungalow and turned into another even narrower one which eventually brought them to the lychgate. Melanie was waiting with David and Mike and a lot of the others when they got there, and as soon as Steve and Sally arrived, they all went up the path between the tombstones and into the cool, dark interior of the church.

The little church was full to the doors for the service that morning, and Tessa enjoyed every minute of it. In fact, had it not been for what had happened at Jamaica Inn, she thought everything would have been quite perfect. Afterwards, coming out in the bright sunlight, she remembered that rain had been forecast, but she hoped it didn't come yet, even though the grown-ups were saying that the farmers were needing it.

There was no sign of it though and the next day was even hotter, and everyone had turned brown as berries. The coolest place was in the sea, so every evening Tessa and the twins would slip down to Trewinth for a swim. Sometimes Jill and Nigel Manners, the twins' friends from down the road, would join them, and either Uncle or Auntie seemed to make a point of going along too. If they couldn't manage it, then Amanda and Sue, two of the beach mission helpers would be there to keep an eye on them — at least Tessa suspected that was what they had been asked to do, for at seventeen, they seemed quite grown up to the children.

On the Tuesday evening, after they had been in for a swim, Sue said 'Why don't we build a sandcastle?' So they all set to work with a will, and with the help of the older girls had soon built a gigantic one.

'Let's put some turrets on it like a real castle,' Peter suggested excitedly, and Nigel said, 'Why don't we make a tunnel through it and dig a moat all round, so that when the sea comes up, it will flow into it!'

The others thought that was a jolly good idea, but Tessa was tired of digging. So she dropped her spade, straightened up, and looked towards the cliff-top, and suddenly there were two men coming down the steep steps in the rock-face. It seemed to Tessa like an intrusion on their privacy, for around this time in the evening they usually had the beach all to themselves, most of the visitors having gone back to their guest-houses. So she stared hard at them as they drew nearer, and suddenly realised that one of them was Mr Jenkins whom she hadn't seen since that awful afternoon last week, which now seemed just like a bad dream to her and much longer ago than seven days.

Seeing him again brought it all back though, and she bit her lip. Then, remembering her manners, she got ready to smile, but to her surprise Mr Jenkins didn't seem to recognise her at first; then when he glanced at her again she thought that he looked a bit taken aback as though embarrassed at seeing her. Though she couldn't imagine why, because the last time they had met, he had been so kind and friendly.

They stopped and chatted for a few minutes, however, Mr Jenkins asking if she and the twins were enjoying their holiday, and introducing his tall companion as 'Mr Trelawney'. So Tessa decided that the stranger must be a relation or friend who was staying with them on holiday — yet she couldn't help noticing that Mr Jenkins seemed rather on edge.

After they had gone on, she stood and watched them as they walked towards the point together, for the tide was going out still and wouldn't be on the turn for a while. Then they disappeared from view around the corner, and her curiosity getting the better of her again, she ran quickly over the smooth sand towards the sea and, hidden from view behind a tall rock, watched the two men walking along the shoreline of the next beach.

Then Amanda was calling to her, and when she looked back, she saw that the others had finished digging and were getting ready to go home. So, with a last look at Mr Jenkins and his friend fast disappearing into the distance, she walked slowly back, telling herself that if they wanted to go for an evening's stroll by the sea, it was none of her business.

'Do you like our sandcastle?' Paula asked as she came up to them, and Jill said it was a pity they couldn't wait until the tide came in so that they could watch it flowing round the moat. Tessa agreed that it was very nice, but she wasn't really thinking about it. Then the four younger children were racing across the beach to the steps, the sandcastle forgotten, but Tessa's mind was still on Mr Jenkins and Mr Trelawney as they all set off across the cliffs for home. So much so, in fact, that whilst the others were busy chattering, she slipped to the cliff edge and peered over. And there, sure enough, were two lonely figures walking slowly along the tide line.

Tessa had nearly forgotten the incident when two evenings later she was down in the cove again watching two gulls fighting over a dead fish. Turning round suddenly she almost collided with a tall figure coming round the point of the adjacent beach. It was Mr Trelawney – on his own this time. He smiled and nodded, though she had an odd sort of a feeling that Mr Jenkins' friend mightn't be particularly pleased to see her – though for the life of her she couldn't think why. So she went on with what she had been doing – which was endeavouring to knock a limpet off a rock for bait for the twins, and tried to put him out of her mind, as he walked away up the beach.

Yet in spite of the vague fears which haunted her from time to time, casting a shadow over her horizon, mostly she forgot them completely when she was with the beach mission crowd. Several of the boys and girls with whom she and Melanie had made friends last week had gone home at the weekend, but more had arrived to take their place, so that by the end of this second week there must have been seventy or eighty of them gathered in front of the sand pulpit each morning.

There were lots of other exciting things to do and places to visit too, and some evenings Auntie and Uncle would take Tessa and the twins by car to one of the little villages further down the coast. Tessa loved to stand and look over the harbour walls at the fishing boats rocking at anchor, and to watch the fishermen sitting mending their nets on the quayside.

One unforgettable evening, they went to Port Isaac, and were fortunate enough to get there just as the Floral Dance was beginning. The local band had been playing down on the harbour plat when they arrived, but now some of the younger folk who knew the steps, formed fours, and then the quaint old Cornish custom began, with the bandsmen blowing out the catchy, familiar tune.

Visitors joined on at the end of the procession, and after a little bit of practice in a corner, Uncle, Tessa and the twins formed a foursome, though Auntie said she would rather watch because she thought she would get in a muddle!

Soon a long column of people stretched all the way up the hill, right to the top of the high street, with visitors lining the pavements on either side, and cameras clicking in all directions. Everyone except the locals seemed to be getting hopelessly mixed up with the foursome in front and the foursome behind, but on they went, undeterred.

By the time they reached the top of the hill, everyone was so out of breath, including the bandsmen, they had to stop for a breather. Then they were off again down the hill in the gathering dusk, the tempo of the music quickening as they drew nearer to the harbour again. Tessa thought she had never laughed so much in all her life as the pace speeded up and everyone got more mixed up than ever. When the crowd broke up later and they all drifted off homewards, the children were so excited, they didn't stop talking until they got back to the bungalow.

Another thing that happened that week was on the Thursday evening after tea, when the twins weren't anywhere to be seen for about three-quarters of an hour. Auntie and Uncle and Tessa searched the house and garden, but there wasn't a sign of them. Uncle rang the Manners, but they hadn't seen them either. So they were all feeling very worried and were just wondering what to do next, when Peter and Paula came walking in through the gate, both looking very excited, though a little guilty, and they both started talking at once.

'We found a nice little lane just back there,' Paula said, pointing down the road, 'and there was a farm with some lovely baby calves and the farmer let us stroke them, and . . .'

'Then we went a bit further down the lane,' Peter chipped in, 'and we found two little cottages. One looked as though someone lived in it, but the other was a bit tumbled down, and we walked all round it and looked in the windows and they were very dirty and cobwebby and . . .'

'. . . and a dog barked at us from one of the windows,' Paula put in, 'and it was quite scary!'

'You might have been trespassing,' Uncle interrupted sternly, 'and the lane you're talking about isn't "just down the road", because there isn't one as near as that, I'm sure! So where have you been?'

'They imagined the whole thing, I expect!' Tessa put in, but the twins looked hurt.

'We didn't imagine it,' Paula said stoutly, but Auntie told them that the next time they wandered off without telling anyone, they would have to go to bed at six o'clock as a punishment.

After that the twins looked rather subdued and crestfallen, but they soon forgot all about it and scampered off to play hide-and-seek in the orchard.

The next afternoon, which was Friday, the Beach Mission party played a game called 'Beating the Tide' which was a firm favourite with almost all the children except Tessa, and could only take place when the sea was coming in. Everyone had to build a sandcastle on the tideline in front of the incoming tide, and sometimes there would be rows and rows of them. Then, when the water came up and surrounded them, you had to jump up on top of your castle, and see how long you could stay there before it got swamped. The winner was the person who stayed up the longest, and obviously the higher you built your castle, the more likely you were to win.

The reason Tessa didn't like the game was because standing on her sandcastle watching the tide rolling towards her reminded her too much of her nasty experience of getting cut off by the tide. So this afternoon she walked over to the far left and took up her position right on the end of the diggers. Everyone started shovelling sand, and after a moment she dropped her spade and looked round to see if anyone was looking. No one was because they were all too busy, and now was the moment to make her escape!

So she moved slowly away towards where the rocks jutted out seawards and found herself mixed up with a party of people who were walking along the beach – which of course couldn't have been better! After that, with another quick glance behind, she broke into a run, congratulating herself that she had got away so easily – for usually she found she couldn't move the length of herself without someone calling to her to do something, or to come here or go there, and sometimes it seemed as though they had got eyes in the backs of their heads! Though she *was* feeling a bit guilty by now!

Next minute, she was round the corner, and looking into a tiny cove which was really just a part of the bigger one, though there wasn't a soul in sight. She was just thinking to herself that she would stroll slowly back, by which time the game would probably be finished, when she was suddenly rooted to the spot with terror as a huge dog appeared on the other side of the cove, snarling and growling and showing its fangs, and rushing full pelt towards her.

As it hurtled nearer, she was certain – for the second time those holidays – that her end had come, when suddenly a voice shouted 'Radar!' and the dog stopped and slunk back towards a tall rock from behind which a short thickset man had appeared. He didn't look very pleased to see her, and he limped as he walked towards her. But she didn't wait to find out more, and took to her heels, trembling like a leaf, and telling herself that it served her right for sneaking off!

When she got back to the others, the sight of a lot of collapsed sandcastles with the sea swirling round them told her that 'Beating the Tide' was over, though to her amazement no-one seemed to have noticed her absence.

Everyone was congratulating Mike, who had been the winner, and then he and David and one or two of the others started kicking a big beachball around. Someone sent it in her direction, but she missed it because her thoughts were still on the man and his dog. For apart from the fact that she had had an awful fright – which she was getting used to by now – she had also had the distinct impression that she had seen the pair of them, the man and his dog, before somewhere, though for the life of her she couldn't think where, and she was still wracking her brains over it as she splashed into the shallows after the brightly coloured ball.

But walking home with the twins half-an-hour later, all at once her mind flashed back to something that had happened last Saturday afternoon when they had been on Bodmin Moor, and suddenly she knew without a shadow of a doubt that the man with his dog 'Radar' she had met in the cove this afternoon, was the same man who had been lurking near their coach at Dozmary Pool, and the dog was the alsatian who had growled at Sheba.

She almost forgot all about the incident however, for when they got back to the bungalow, they found that Auntie had kept her promise and there was a lovely lobster salad waiting for them.

Saturday came round again and it was time for the second barbecue, to which everyone had been eagerly looking forward all week. That evening they lit the bonfire right on the edge of the low cliff that sloped down to a little cove on the other side of Poltuan. They cooked sausages over the flames and hot-dogs were doled out by the dozen. There were lots of other lovely things to eat too, including vol-au-vents, sandwiches, sausage rolls, cake and biscuits, with squash to wash it all down and fruit salad and ice-cream afterwards. Sheba was running around eagerly, on the look out for any tit-bits that might come her way.

After supper they played beach games and swam, and

about nine o'clock, David said, 'How about a walk to the top of the cliff?' So he and Tessa and Melanie, with a few of the others crossed the beach to climb the steep path on the opposite side of the cove. It was quite a way to the top, but when they got there, they were rewarded with a lovely view all along the coast. A fishing boat with its lonely occupant rocked at anchor in the bay, and as the sun went down and dusk began to fall, the rugged outlines became black and mysterious, and everyone fell silent, because it was so breathtaking. Brilliant shades of red and orange streaked the darkening sky before the sun disappeared below the horizon and Tessa thought it was the most beautiful sunset she had ever seen.

Everything was very still and all they could hear was the murmur of the sea on the pebbles in the cove below, for the ocean was calm as a millpond, except when a gull or cormorant swooped down after a fish and there was a faint plop, or the occasional crackle of the bonfire came to their ears, or the sound of voices from the other side of the cove.

Out in the bay, the fishing-boat was almost invisible now and they could only just make out the figure of the fisherman as he leant over the side hauling up the last of his lobster-pots. To the left and a little behind them, a disused tin-mine rose stark and eerie on the headland, silhouetted against the night sky and suddenly someone suggested that they go over and have a look at it.

'OK' David agreed, 'So long as you don't fall down the shaft!' and Tessa sprang eagerly to her feet, for she had been dying to get near to one ever since she had first seen them dotted around the landscape. The others were equally keen, so they all walked towards it over the springy turf and close to it looked huge and quite awesome. They strolled all round it, viewing it from every side and peering down into the blackness of the shaft which seemed bottomless. As she gazed at it, little did Tessa suspect that the next time she stood close to the mine, it would be in very different circumstances.

By now it was time for them to rejoin the rest of the party, so they found the cliff path again and started walking back. Tessa was lagging behind everyone else, reluctant to leave as she stared out over the darkening sea. Then she didn't know what made her do it, but when the others were nearly at the bottom of the hill, she turned round for a last look at the tin-mine standing grim and desolate and almost invisible now against the dark back-cloth of the sky. All at once her heart gave a sickening lurch and the panic feelings which were becoming so familiar nowadays came over her again. For as she looked, it seemed to her that a tall figure had detached itself from the shadows and she was absolutely certain that there was someone standing up there on the cliff-top beside the tin-mine, staring down at her. Seconds later when she looked again, she could see nothing.

Her knees still felt wobbly as she caught up with the others, and she glanced uncertainly at David wondering whether she ought to tell him. But he was talking to Mike, and she didn't like to butt in because it *could* have been her imagination: she had been ever so jumpy since the Jamaica Inn incident.

So they joined the others — nearly one hundred of them sitting around the dying embers of the fire in the semi-dusk as they sang their favourite hymns and choruses. Steve gave a short epilogue, after which there was a closing prayer, and then they were dousing the bonfire and packing everything up.

Making tracks for home, Tessa still felt nervous and took good care to keep close to the others as they walked back across the cliffs to the village. For she was sure by now that the two mysterious young men who had crossed her path on two occasions were the escaped convicts!

9: Lost and Found

Tessa awoke bright and early next morning, her fears of the previous evening almost forgotten in the realisation that it was Sunday and therefore a very special day. She had so enjoyed going to St Cuthbert's last week and joining in the service in the little old church on the cliff. The only fly in the ointment was that they had come to the final week of the Beach Mission.

Later, as they sat packed in like sardines waiting for the service to begin, she studied the elaborately carved choir-stalls and pew ends and looked at the beautiful rich colours in the stained glass window over the Communion Table, wishing as she did so that Melanie who was sitting next to her, wasn't going home at the end of the week, for they had become such good friends by now that she would miss her a lot.

She tried to forget about that though, and stared out through the plain glass window on the other side of the aisle, to where fields full of Friesian cows and sheep stretched away to the coastline and the blue of the Atlantic Ocean. There was that funny musty smell too, which reminded her of how long this tiny building had stood here on the top of the cliff in all winds and weather, and of all the people who had worshipped in it over the years.

All the team were there – Steve, Barry, Sally and the other helpers, most of whom were in their late teens and early twenties, and who had given up their summer holidays to come and help, several of whom she had got to know very well, including, of course, Amanda and Sue. Auntie and Uncle were here this morning too, and Tessa was glad about that.

Then there was a brief commotion, when one of the twins — sitting up near the front — dropped their collection, and it went rolling under the pews. They spent the next few minutes grovelling on the floor out of sight, until they eventually emerged triumphant, the coin held aloft for all to see, which made everybody smile. Then the choir entered, with the Vicar bringing up the rear and the service began.

The first lesson — the Old Testament reading — was taken from the first chapter of Genesis, and was about the Creation; the second came from the New Testament and was the story of the Prodigal Son. Everyone followed in their pew Bibles and then they sang some of the choruses which they had come to know so well, and after that there was a talk for the younger ones on the Parable of the Sower, which was illustrated with a flannelgraph.

After the next hymn, the Vicar gave them all a warm welcome again, but Tessa felt a lump in her throat when it got to the part where he gave a special one to the Beach Mission. For he said that, sadly, it was for the last time, which reminded her that everyone would be on their way home next Saturday, and that made her feel quite miserable. Though she cheered up at the thought that there was still another week to look forward to, and Melanie whispered to her that the last one was always the best!

Then she remembered that ten days after that she and the twins would be going home too, in time for the start of the autumn term. How sorry she would be to leave Cornwall, she thought, and how she would miss the Jenkins and Sheba — though Auntie had said that she and the twins could come and stay whenever they liked, so that was something to look forward to anyway.

She thought too of the letter she had received from

Mummy yesterday morning, telling her that she and Daddy were feeling much better and well on the way to recovery . . . and then she switched her mind back to the present for the notices were over and they were standing to sing another hymn. Later in the service, the Vicar went into the pulpit and talked about the Prodigal Son. The picture he painted was so vivid that she could see it all quite clearly in her mind's eye.

They were all, he said, like the Prodigal Son – away in the far country of sin – until they returned to their Heavenly Father. That was, he explained, the meaning of the long word 'repentance' – coming to God and claiming forgiveness through faith in His son, Jesus Christ.

At the end of the service they rose to sing the final hymn which was *Stand up, stand up for Jesus, ye soldiers of the Cross* which seemed to Tessa a very appropriate one, because many of them would be going back to homes which were not Christian, and to schools where their friends didn't share their faith. And that would mean they would need to remember to pray and read their Bibles every day and attend church and Sunday School regularly, if they were to stand firm.

Then they were all filing out of the cool church into the bright sunshine, and the Vicar was standing outside to shake hands with everyone. Auntie and Uncle joined Tessa and Melanie and they walked down the path between the leaning tombstones to the lychgate, the twins running on ahead with Nigel and Jillie – and Tessa made up her mind that she would come back sometime – if possible on her own – and have a look around the churchyard.

As it happened, she returned sooner than she expected, for during lunch, just as they were starting on their banana splits Tessa noticed with horror that her gold bracelet which Mummy and Daddy had given her for her birthday, wasn't on her wrist. She jumped up, the spoon half-way to her mouth exclaiming, 'Oh! my bracelet's gone!'

'Oh Tessa!' Auntie said, and the others stared at her in dismay. Then they were all peering under the table and walking all round the dining-room looking on the floor. But it wasn't there. Tessa ran out into the hall and upstairs to her bedroom, but there was no sign of it. So she walked slowly downstairs again, feeling very miserable, and Auntie told her to sit down and finish her meal and then they would have a look in the garden to see if she had dropped it on the path.

But it wasn't there either – she tried hard to remember when she had last seen it on her wrist, and the more she thought about it, the more sure she was that it had been there whilst she was in the church. So it must be lying somewhere between here and St Cuthbert's.

'I'll just walk up the lane and have a look,' she told Auntie who had started clearing the table, and the twins jumped up and said they would go with her. So they went out through the gate and across the road, eyes glued to the ground, and turned into the lane opposite, but though they looked under almost every blade of grass, they couldn't see the bracelet.

So they walked on and into the other lane with high hedges on either side which led to the church, and when they reached the lychgate, they saw an oldish car parked a little way away, under the shade of some trees which bordered the churchyard. They went through the gate for the second time in two hours and up the path towards the porch, and Tessa couldn't help feeling very worried and miserable, though she was praying hard that they would find her bracelet, and so were the twins.

She had almost given up all hope by the time they entered the shadowy porch, for it seemed perfectly certain by now that someone must have come along and found it lying in the lane and picked it up – and unless they happened to be honest and had handed it in at the police-station, she knew she would never see it again, and whatever would Mummy say!

She was just going to turn the big iron ring on the heavy old door to go inside the church, when Paula who was just behind her, called out 'Tess!' excitedly, and Tessa swung round to see her young sister squatting down on the stone floor, peering underneath one of the long stone benches which ran along either side of the porch. Next minute she had straightened up, her hand raised high in triumph as she held the bracelet aloft.

'It must have fallen off your wrist as you came out of church Tessie,' she said with sparkling eyes, 'and rolled underneath out of sight!'

'Oh *thank* you, Paula!' Tessa said delightedly, and Peter said 'Jolly good,' and gave his twin a brotherly slap on the back by way of congratulation. Tessa took the bracelet from her sister, her face wreathed in smiles, and slipped it back over her hand, fastening the clasp and gazing down at it with relief, for she had been so sure she would never see it again. She must get Mummy to take it to the jewellers when she got back home though for if there was something wrong with the clasp, the same thing might happen again.

They went out into the churchyard again then, Paula skipping on ahead and calling out to Peter, 'Let's have a look round the other side,' and the two youngsters scampered off to the left, while Tessa walked in the opposite direction, even though at the back of her mind she had a feeling they ought to go straight back and tell Auntie and Uncle that all was well, so that they wouldn't worry any more.

We won't be long though, she thought, and stepped off the path onto the grass, to walk between one of the long rows of neat tombstones.

It was very quiet and peaceful in the little churchyard,

with butterflies flitting about amongst the flowers on the graves – the silence broken only by the buzzing of a bee in the honeysuckle, the scent of which wafted over from a nearby hedge, and the murmur of the twins' voices not far off. Everything seemed just perfect in fact, and Tessa felt so grateful that her prayer had been answered again and that she had her bracelet back.

She went on a little further and in front of her was a big oblong tomb, standing quite high like a table. It stood beneath the shade of a clump of trees almost up against the hedge, which had a small gap in it at that point. As she went nearer, Tessa noticed that there was writing all round the sides of the tomb, and she paused, fascinated, trying to make out the names and dates which were very faint because it was so old. The lettering was almost worn away in places, or else it was so covered over with lichen that all she could make out were the figures sixteen hundred and something, the rest being completely unreadable.

'What a funny old tomb,' she said aloud.

Then she wandered round to the back of the tomb to see what it looked like from the other side, where under the shade of the overhanging trees it was suddenly chilly, so that she shivered. There was a space about two feet wide between the big oblong block and the hedge, and as she stood looking down at the soil, she noticed that it looked newly trodden as though someone had walked over it several times recently, and at the same time she had the uncanny feeling that she was not alone!

Miles away, she was jerked back to reality by the sound of a heavy footstep in the lane immediately behind her and the hedge, followed by a rustling of leaves and the snapping of a twig – and sensing a presence she swung round, her heart leaping into her throat, and there was a man looking down at her! He was tall, with dark matted black hair and there was another one just behind him – shorter and with slitty eyes – and she knew at once who they were!

Next minute the tall man's hand shot out and seized her in a grip of steel – and she remembered thinking that it was her arm this time – not her shoulder. She opened her mouth to speak but no words came and she wondered in a hazy, unreal sort of way whether the twins would get captured too or whether they would be able to raise the alarm.

Then the man jerked her towards him, and said in a rasping undertone,

'Keep out of this, d'you understand! If yer don't, it'll be the worse for you!'

10: The Mystery Deepens

What happened next was unbelievable, for Tessa heard the sound of heavy footsteps again — this time on the gravel path — and someone was hurrying towards them. At the same time a pleasant voice called out, 'Hey, what's going on here?' and next minute Tessa's captor had let go of her arm, pushing her roughly from him so that she pitched headlong to the ground.

After that there was the sound of more footsteps — thudding off down the lane behind her this time — followed seconds later by the noise of a car revving up and the roar of its engine as it gradually faded into the distance. Then the pleasant voice spoke again.

'Got their number anyway!' it said a bit breathlessly, and Tessa stared dazedly into the face of its owner who was bending over her with a kind smile and helping her to her feet. As he did so, she remembered in a hazy, distant sort of way that she had seen him before somewhere, though she couldn't think where.

'Are you all right?' her rescuer asked anxiously as he searched her face with his keen grey eyes, and she nodded, quite unable to speak, but knowing suddenly who he was.

'The twins!' she gasped fearfully, finding her voice at last. 'Where are the twins?' and she stood shakily beside the tomb, rubbing her arm where the man had grabbed it, for it felt a bit sore. Then she saw them — standing on the grass a little way away — hands clasped tightly, faces pale beneath their tan, eyes like saucers — and looking scared out of their wits.

Mr Trelawney—for that was who it was—looked surprised as he said, 'So the twins are here too! I thought you were on your own, Tessa,' and he looked down at her white face and then at her arm and asked for the second time if she was all right. Tessa nodded again, blinking back the tears and swallowing hard as she brushed the soil from her dress which was quite dirty from where she had fallen, and Mr Trelawney called out to Peter and Paula, 'Don't worry twins! Tessa isn't hurt!'

As he said it, Tessa felt a twinge of surprise at the back of her mind that Mr Trelawney should have remembered her name, but there were other and more important matters to think about and she whispered to him, 'Who . . . who *are* they?' adding after a slight pause, 'And what do they want with *me*?' and waited breathlessly for him to speak.

Mr Trelawney didn't answer her question, but instead he asked her another one, placing a comforting hand on her arm.

'Did they say anything to you, Tessa?'

'Yes,' she whispered faintly, 'They said, "Y-you k-keep out of this"—or something, and if not they s-said it w-would be the worse for me . . . Wh-what did they mean, Mr Trelawney?' she asked stutteringly.

Again he didn't answer, merely asking whether she had ever seen them before, whereupon she told him that she had—twice—on the beach that awful Tuesday, and then again at Jamaica Inn. When she had finished speaking he put a fatherly arm around her shoulders.

'Try not to worry about them, Tessa. We know what they look like now, anyway!' which didn't tell her very much. Then he was leading her towards the twins.

'Who *were* those horrid men?' Peter and Paula demanded as they came up to Tessa and Mr Trelawney, but all Mr Trelawney said was 'Hello, twins! What a good thing I happened to come along—just at the right moment!' Then he put an arm around them too and was leading them all off in the direction of the lychgate and Tessa murmured, 'Whatever would have happened if you hadn't?' and tried hard not to think about it.

'My car's outside,' Mr Trelawney said next, 'and I'm going to run you all home,' and then he started talking about the weather and their holiday to take their minds off what had happened and they climbed into his big shiny car which stood by the lychgate and sat in the back whilst he got into the driver's seat and started up the engine. Tessa knew they were quite safe with him at any rate, if he was a friend of the Jenkins – at least she hoped they were. Everything was so confusing!

They moved off, gliding smoothly along the narrow lane, and Mr Trelawney surprised Tessa again by saying, 'Let me see, it's No. 6 Tremayne Road, isn't it?' and Tessa said that it was, wondering how he knew. Whilst the twins, refusing to be side-tracked, demanded to know again who the nasty men were.

'We shall know soon, I'm sure,' Mr Trelawney said soothingly, his eyes on the road ahead, and then they turned the corner and there was their bungalow. He got out and opened the car door for them and the children all tumbled out, Tessa remembering that she hadn't thanked their rescuer properly yet. So she clutched his arm and said gratefully, '*Thank* you, Mr Trelawney,' and she didn't ask who the men were again or what they wanted, or indeed what it was that she was supposed to keep out of – for she had the feeling that even if he knew, he wouldn't tell her.

'A pleasure, my dear!' he said, smiling kindly down at her, and went to push open the gate for them as though he intended coming in too – though if she hadn't been so upset, Tessa would have asked him in anyway, so that Uncle and Auntie could meet him and thank him too.

They all walked up the path together, the twins whispering in subdued voices, and Tessa led the way round to the garden door at the back of the bungalow. Now that some of the numbness and shock were beginning to wear off a little, she found herself wondering what Mr Trelawney himself had been doing in the churchyard. She would very much have liked to know, but decided it would be better not to embarrass him by asking any more questions which he obviously didn't want to answer. And though it was very annoying to be kept guessing, she would just have to trust him and hope that she would be told something soon.

They walked through the garden door into the lounge; and as they did so, Auntie and Uncle came in to the room by the other door and looked relieved to see them, but a little startled when Mr Trelawney followed them in. Yet it was Tessa's turn to be surprised when they said, 'Hello, Mr Trelawney,' just as though they knew him quite well. Then Uncle started to explain that he and Auntie had been just setting out to look for them and they hadn't realised that the time had gone by so quickly. For after they had left, Mummy had 'phoned up from London for a chat, and had wanted to speak to both him and Auntie, and she had only just rung off.

There was an awkward little pause after that, during which the atmosphere seemed rather tense, and Auntie and Uncle looked at the twins – unusually silent and subdued – and at Tessa with her dress all dirty and her hair awry, and still looking pale and anxious. Then they glanced enquiringly at Mr Trelawney who in turn looked at Tessa rather apologetically and asked her if she would mind taking the twins out into the garden for a few minutes, though he smiled so nicely when he said it that Tessa couldn't feel offended, even though she knew they weren't wanted just then.

So she piloted the children towards the door again and then remembered that she hadn't said anything about her bracelet. So she went back and told them how Paula had found it under the stone seat in the church porch, and suddenly remembering that she hadn't explained to Mr Trelawney how she came to be in the churchyard in the first place, she put him in the picture about that too.

'So glad you found it anyway dear,' Auntie told her, and then she and the twins went out into the garden and left the grown-ups on their own, but none of the children felt like talking very much because they were all too busy wondering what it was that Mr Trelawney was saying to Uncle and Auntie that he couldn't say in front of them.

They didn't have long to wait though, for presently the three grown-ups came out onto the path and stood chatting, and Tessa thought that perhaps *now* they would be told something. But instead Mr Trelawney merely turned towards them with a wave and a smile and a cheerful, 'Goodbye Tessa! Goodbye twins! See you sometime!' and next minute he was walking away round the corner of the bungalow and she heard the sound of his car starting up.

Disappointed, she stood listening to the noise of the engine dying away into the distance, and then Auntie was calling across the lawn, 'Just going to make you nice hot drinks to buck you up, children,' whilst Uncle came and sat down in a deckchair and asked Tessa how she felt after her adventure – though she knew he didn't have any intention of telling her anything. So she and the twins sipped their hot milk and though she was dying to ask questions, she didn't because by now she was beginning to get rather tired of being treated like a baby and not told anything. Auntie and Uncle were obviously making a great effort to behave normally and as though nothing out-of-the-ordinary had happened, but Tessa guessed that they must be terribly worried.

'How clever of you, Paula, to find Tessa's bracelet,' Uncle remarked, trying to sound cheerful. But when the twins had run off to the orchard for a swing, he said very seriously that Tessa and the twins mustn't go off on their own any more, and that in future he or Auntie would come with them. That made Tessa ask anxiously whether it would make any difference to their going along to the Beach Mission, but to her relief he said they could still go because they wouldn't be on their own there. So with that she had to be content.

However, during the week that followed, things seemed to go on very much as before, though Tessa did feel rather worried by something that happened on the Monday evening after the churchyard episode. She was playing on the lawn when she accidentally overheard Auntie and Uncle talking together in the lounge with the garden door wide open, and though she hadn't intended to eavesdrop, she couldn't help hearing the first part of what they were saying. It sounded very much as though they were thinking of sending the twins and herself home early, and though she didn't stop to hear any more, she kept expecting after that to be told to pack her things in readiness for immediate departure. But the days went by and nothing more was said about it, for which she was truly thankful. Having to leave Cornwall early would have been almost worse than anything, she thought.

Melanie knew all about everything by now – at least as much as Tessa knew – because her friend hadn't felt she could leave her in the dark about things any longer when it was quite obvious she knew that something peculiar was going on. Of course, Melanie was horrified when Tessa told her, which made her wonder whether she had been wise to frighten her unnecessarily. But she was very impressed by the way in which her rescue from the beach had come about, and that it had resulted in her attending the beach services and becoming a Christian. And of course, Melanie thought that Tessa's escape in the churchyard last Sunday had been absolutely amazing. Tessa confided in her that she was sure of one thing anyway – and that was that the two men were wanted by the police for something. In fact, she told Melanie, she thought they were the convicts! She also mentioned that she had an idea that Mr Trelawney was none other than a plain clothes detective – though what he had been doing in the churchyard, she couldn't imagine, and Auntie and Uncle changed the subject every time she mentioned it!

Anyway, there didn't seem much that either of them could do about it, except pray every day that the men would soon be caught and that Tessa and the twins would be kept safe from further trouble. In spite of everything that had happened, Tessa didn't worry about it *all* the time. In fact, sometimes she almost forgot about it altogether for the time being, particularly when they were having fun surfing, swimming, playing games and going off on lovely excursions to places like Land's End, the Lizard and Kynance Cove. At times like that, it almost seemed as though all the nasty things that had happened were just a bad dream.

The beach mission crowd were so kind too, and Tessa was sure that Steve and Sally and the others knew something at least of what was going on – yet when she had mentioned it to them one day after the beach service, they had been strangely silent, just like everyone else! It must have been a terrible worry for them all, Tessa thought, yet her third week with the Beach Mission party was just as enjoyable – if not more so – than the first two. The twins had been warned to say nothing to their friends about last Sunday afternoon, so as to avoid creating panic amongst the younger children, and Tessa knew they were keeping their promise not to talk about it, for they were getting much better at that sort of thing these days than they used to be.

It didn't rain at all so that by the end of that last week they had had a month of continuous sunshine and Tessa's hair was bleached to a platinum blonde colour. Nothing else alarming occurred, so she began to think that perhaps the two men had gone away from the neighbourhood altogether. Yet when she ventured to ask David if there was any news of them, he had shrugged and shaken his head, looking suddenly serious, so that she knew she had been wrong and they were still around.

They had a record attendance of well over one hundred at the beach service on the last Friday, though nothing had been arranged for the afternoon, as everyone would be busy packing to go home the next day. Melanie went round to tea with Tessa in the afternoon as it was her last day, and though they would both miss each other very much, for they had become great friends by now, they had promised to write regularly and Melanie was going to let Tessa know all about the new school she was going to next term. As she, like Tessa, had been staying with relations, and came to Cornwall every summer, there was a good chance that they would meet each other here next year too.

What was more, the two girls heard a piece of interesting news on the six o'clock news that evening, which made them sit up and take notice. The announcer gave out at the end that the two convicts who had escaped from Dartmoor prison had been captured that very morning, down near Penzance. Tessa breathed a sigh of relief when she heard that, for she was quite certain by now that they were the two who had deserted her on the beach, as well as giving her a fright at Jamaica Inn. Now that they were caught, she told herself, there wouldn't be any need to worry any more.

So she and Melanie went off happily to the Beach Mission headquarters – which was the big granite house Tessa had first seen on the Saturday afternoon when they had rescued Sheba – for a final 'squash' before everyone went home the next day. She had already been inside it on two or three occasions, and at seven o'clock everyone crowded into the front room which faced the sea, and because there were so many of them, they overflowed onto the stairs in the hall.

First there were sandwiches, sausage rolls and home-made cakes, with squash and trifles and lots of ice-cream, and after that everyone sat down – on chairs if they could find them, otherwise on the floor or the stairs – for a sing-song and the final epilogue – choosing all their favourite choruses and doing the actions where appropriate, and feeling rather sad because it was for the last time, and tomorrow most of them would have gone their separate ways. In fact, everyone felt quite envious of Tessa and the twins because they had another ten days to go.

They finished with a last, rousing hymn, and then they all said goodbye to one another, and Steve and Sally – who everyone suspected were going to get engaged before long! – promised to write to Tessa and keep in touch with her, which cheered her up considerably. Sally also gave her the name and address of a Bible Class leader who ran a class near Tessa's home, and who happened to be a friend of hers. She would give Tessa a warm welcome to it if she went along, she assured her – and the twins too, for which Tessa was very grateful.

* * *

For the first day or two after the departure of all their friends, Tessa couldn't help feeling rather lost and forlorn, and everything seemed a bit flat. Though they soon got used to it and of course there was always David and Sheba for company, and the twins could still play with Nigel and Jillie.

The weather had turned a lot cooler now, for summer was fast going, and in the early mornings there was already a feeling of autumn in the air, and the evenings were drawing in. Tessa felt sorry that the long, hot days were over, though she liked the autumn too, when the woods were full of mellow bronzes, golds and browns, and the leaves were turning on the trees. Even winter could be nice, with its cold, crisp days, its cosy evenings round the fireside and the magic of Christmas.

The beaches and cliffs were becoming more and more deserted now, for most of the visitors had gone home, but Tessa and the twins still went swimming in Trewinth Cove. Sometimes she and Peter and Paula would go round to the Coastguard Cottage for tea, and they would spend the evening there – and Tessa enjoyed these visits, for Mr Jenkins would talk about his experiences as a coastguard and she would sit on the floor for an hour or more, her arm around Sheba's neck, listening enthralled as he told tales of some of the exciting sea rescue operations he had taken part in.

The final day of the holidays arrived at last. Tessa had neither seen nor heard anything of the two men for nearly three weeks now, which made her more sure than ever that her theory about the convicts had been right, but all the same she had the feeling that Auntie and Uncle would be very relieved when she and the twins were safely back home with Mummy and Daddy – though she would be sorry to part with them, of course. They must have been terribly worried, knowing all about what was going on, Tessa thought, and she didn't suppose they would really feel able to relax until they were all safely back home, after everything that had happened.

Yet she still wasn't sure what it was all about, except that two people who were wanted by the police had a grudge against her, though for the life of her she couldn't think why they should have picked on her – and she was beginning to think, what's more, that she never *would* get to the bottom of it. For even now that the convicts had been caught, still nobody would tell her anything!

It was all very puzzling and her head ached sometimes with thinking about it. Yet in the end, it wasn't she but the twins who got the worst of it, and all because they had been with her in the churchyard that Sunday afternoon.

11: Tessa Learns the Truth

Tessa awoke that last morning with mixed feelings, for she was sorry to be leaving this lovely place which had come to mean so much to her. Yet at the same time she was looking forward to seeing Daddy and Mummy again, and all her school-friends the following week when she went back to school.

She spent the morning packing and helping the twins to pack, and in the afternoon she had been invited round to tea at the Coastguard Cottage for the last time. The twins had also been asked, but they had decided at the last minute to go next door but one and play with Jill and Nigel who were great friends of theirs by now. Auntie had meanwhile gone off to Bodmin for the afternoon to do some shopping.

Mr Jenkins was down at the coastguard station when Tessa arrived, but Mrs Jenkins had prepared a lovely tea for her, with splits and strawberry jam and lashings of Cornish cream, which of course she had already sampled many times during this holiday. There were delicious meringues and other home-made cakes to follow and afterwards Tessa helped with the washing-up. When they had cleared up Mrs Jenkins suggested that she and David take Sheba for a walk on the cliff, whilst she got on with some ironing.

So the two of them set off along the cliff path in a northerly direction, accompanied by the spaniel, until presently they came to the little cove where the barbecue had taken place. It was quite deserted now and silent — except for the plaintive mewing of the gulls and the gentle murmur of the sea, and as they approached, the little groups of dunlin which had been running about in the seaweed at the water's edge, fluttered off in fright. They climbed down the low grass-covered cliff onto the beach, and Tessa felt quite sad suddenly, because she was seeing it all for the last time.

David picked up a handful of pebbles and with a deft flick of his wrist sent them skimming out one by one over the flat, calm sea. Then Tessa had a go, but she hadn't got the knack of it, and hers—instead of bouncing—just went straight to the bottom of the ocean, so that David laughed at her. He tried to show her how it was done, but she wasn't concentrating because she had other and more important matters on her mind—for she was going home tomorrow and before she went she just had to know about those two men who had haunted her.

So she went and sat down on a flat slab of rock near Sheba, who was very attached to her by now, and stroked her soft coat and felt even sadder because she would be leaving her behind too. Then she took a deep breath and plunged straight in with what was on her mind, without anything leading up to it. And she noticed a startled expression spring into David's eyes as she asked pleadingly 'Those two men *were* the convicts, weren't they, David? Though nobody will tell me anything even now they ... they've been caught! And ... and why were they so interested in *me*?' Yet even as she spoke the words, a sudden doubt had sprung into her mind, and she looked quickly at David who had stopped throwing stones and wore a thoughtful expression on his sunburnt face.

There was a little silence after that, during which all she could hear was the hammering of her heart against her ribs, and she thought for a moment he wasn't going to answer her questions. Then he looked at her and said firmly—as though he had just made up his mind about something—

'No, they weren't the convicts. The convicts have been found, as you know ... I suppose I might as well tell you though, Tess. We've kept it from you all this time because we didn't want to alarm you and the twins and spoil your holiday. But as you're going home tomorrow, it doesn't really matter any more,' and he sent another stone bouncing out over the water.

Tessa began to get impatient then and burst out, 'Then who *were* they? ... They were wanted by the police for something, weren't they?' and when he nodded, she went on excitedly, 'And Mr Trelawney was a plain-clothes detective, wasn't he?'

'Correct first time,' David teased and she could see she was going to have to winkle it out of him, for he still didn't seem in a hurry to tell her who they were.

'And have *they* been caught too?' she asked eagerly, 'whoever they are,' but he shook his head and Tessa waited breathlessly for him to tell her more.

'Not yet, I'm afraid, but the police have got plenty of clues and they hope to get them very soon. There's a twenty-four hour watch being kept around the coast, only what with the convicts too, they've been rather busy just lately!'

Tessa's eyes widened, and suddenly – dramatically – the truth dawned upon her in a flash. Round the coast! Why on earth had she never thought of it before, though the convicts had rather put *her* off the scent too.

'They're smugglers!' she said, sitting bolt upright, and at the same moment she turned to look up at the top of the cliff – the one they had climbed that Saturday evening, where the tin-mine stood gaunt against the skyline. And at that moment she forgot everything else for the time begin because of the amazing discovery she had just made that the two men who had haunted her for the past four weeks were nothing less than real live smugglers! Which was even more exciting than convicts! Why hadn't she guessed?

So she looked up at David again and he nodded, and she burst out eagerly, 'I'd forgotten there were smugglers about these days — I mean I knew there were in olden times of course. What are they smuggling — stolen money?'

'Cannabis!' David said grimly, and a startled look sprang into Tessa's eyes, and they widened in amazement.

'Cannabis!' she repeated with a gasp — and now that she knew, she wondered why on earth she had never thought of *that* before either! How dim she had been!

'Yes,' David said, more willing to talk now that the truth was out. 'It's a rotten business. The stuff's being hidden all along this part of the coast, and . . .'

'In the caves!' Tessa shouted in triumph to the seagulls, and everything began to slot into place and became crystal clear, and in her mind's eye, Tessa saw again the two men coming out of the big cavern in the cliff-face, and remembered the look they had given her when they realised she was there and they were not alone. Smuggling cannabis! It all seemed so obvious now.

'Yes,' David said, looking at a guillemot perched on a nearby rock with its wings outstretched to dry off. 'That day when you first saw them, they had dumped the stuff the previous night as usual and had just come back to check that everything was OK. After you told us what had happened and Dad had taken you home, I went straight back to the beach as soon as the tide was low enough, to have a look for myself.'

'And you found the cannabis?' Tessa asked, her pulses racing.

'Yes, quite a lot of it, tucked away right at the back of the cave in tin boxes.'

'Oh!' Tessa was silent for a moment, hearing only the ebb and flow of the tide on the pebbles. And she was transported back suddenly to the cold dark interior of the cave, alone with the plop, plop of water from the roof. If she had gone on a bit further, she would have seen those boxes for herself ... and then what would the men have done to her? She gave an involuntary shudder, for it didn't bear thinking about.

'Yes, you had a lucky escape, Tessa,' David said seriously, and she guessed that her thoughts had been mirrored on her face. 'The police came and seized the lot that night and set a watch,' he went on after a moment, 'but the men must have got wind of what had happened, for they didn't turn up there again, and we realised they must have found some other hiding place.'

'What were your father and Mr Trelawney doing on the beach in the evenings? I met them twice at Trewinth – at least Mr Trelawney twice – and they didn't seem very pleased to see me,' and Tessa frowned as she waited for David to answer, for it was something that had puzzled her a lot.

'They were keeping an eye on things in general – and you in particular,' David told her, 'only they didn't want you to suspect that was what they were doing!'

The pieces were beginning to fit into place now like a jigsaw puzzle, but she still couldn't see where she came into it all and she said so.

'Ah well you see,' David explained, 'You were there that Tuesday afternoon all on your own on that lonely beach, which is completely inaccessible except at low tide. You were looking into a cave and so I suppose they immediately became suspicious and decided you must be snooping on them. I mean, they probably thought you would never have been there all by yourself unless the police had sent you because they were using you to spy on them and smell out their hidey-holes.'

'Oh, I *see*!' Tessa exclaimed as everything became clear. 'I never thought of *that* either!'

'Well, you wouldn't, would you,' David said with his old familiar grin. 'I mean you came down to Cornwall for a holiday – not to get mixed up with smugglers – or convicts either, for that matter!'

'All the same, it was a silly idea of theirs,' Tessa said frowning. 'As if the police would . . .'

'I know,' David interrupted. 'But still, it was possible, I suppose. Someone your age wouldn't give the game away so much. And then of course you and I were together a lot and they knew you were friendly with Mum and Dad. They were probably watching us hundreds of times! And they would know Dad's the coastguard, and the Beach Mission could just have been a cover up. In any case, you were a danger to them, because for all they knew you had seen those tin boxes in that cave.'

'Hm . . .' Tessa said, twisting her long blonde hair around her finger as she gazed towards the horizon. Then she went on after a short pause, 'Jamaica Inn! That must have made them really suspicious – they must have been convinced we were in league then,' and she shivered as another thought came into her mind. 'What were they doing in the churchyard that afternoon?' she asked.

'Ah well! As the caves were becoming a bit dodgy, they had to find somewhere else, and that table-like tomb was ideal for their purpose because the back comes away and it's empty inside and there's a lot of room in it. As a matter of fact, it was used by smugglers in the olden days – and that's pretty well known around these parts, although the men probably wouldn't have realised that. So the police decided to investigate and Mr Trelawney had just popped in for a look round that Sunday afternoon – fortunately!'

'Yes, and after what you've told me, I can see that it must have looked very suspicious, my standing there in the churchyard looking at the back of that old tomb!'

'It must have made them dead sure they were right,' David agreed.

They didn't say anything for a moment, but just stared at a row of cormorants sitting on a rock out to sea—and Tessa thought again of everything that had happened in the last four weeks. A fishing boat drifted into view just then and dropped anchor, and they watched as its solitary occupant leaned over the side and started to haul on a thick piece of rope. David broke the silence to explain that he was getting in his lobster-pots and there would probably be quite a lot of lobsters and crabs inside. Tessa felt sorry for the poor things and wondered whether it was the same little boat they had watched from the cliff that night of the barbecue.

'And they're still around?' she asked, coming back to the all-important topic, and she shivered again, for the evenings were growing quite chilly now.

'We seem to have lost track of them at the moment. They may have moved on to another part of Cornwall . . . Come on, Tessa! Come on, Sheba! We'd better be getting back before it gets dark,' he said, and whistled to the spaniel.

Sheba bounded over to them from the other side of the cove, glad to be on the move again, and they climbed to the top of the low cliff and set off along the path for home. But as they did so, Tessa turned her head for a last look along the coast, where fields stretched dimly away as far as the eye could see, and foam washed the bottom of the cliffs, white against the greying sea. And she remembered with a pang that tomorrow she was going home—which she had almost forgotten for the time being in the excitement of what she had just been told. The thought made her quite sad—and besides, she *would* have liked to know what happened about the smugglers . . . and perhaps now she never would.

Then she glanced back again—but this time upwards—to the top of the cliff on the other side, where the tin-mine stood shadowy against the waning light. And as she stared at it, half fearfully, she remembered with a thrill of excitement something that for the time being she had half-forgotten, and which she must tell David at once.

12: Where are the Twins?

'David,' Tessa began slowly, 'do you remember that evening of the barbecue when some of us climbed to the top of that cliff?' She nodded back over her shoulder as she said it, and something in the tone of her voice caught David's attention, and he glanced quickly at her.

'Yes,' he answered curiously. 'Why?'

'Do you remember going up to look at the tin-mine?' she asked him, and they both stopped dead in the middle of the path and turned to gaze up at it. 'Well, as we were all coming back down the hill, I was walking behind everybody else, and when we were about half-way down, I happened to look back and it was getting dark and . . .'

'And what?' David interrupted eagerly, for it was his turn to be impatient now.

'I'm sure there was somebody up there . . . somebody tall standing at the side of the tin-mine looking down at us! I was scared stiff, only . . .'

'Why didn't you tell me?' David said excitedly. 'Someone standing by the tin-mine . . .' he repeated, and a startled look sprang into his eyes and he drew in his breath and whistled.

'One minute there wasn't anything there, and the next minute there was! Something seemed to step out of the shadows,' Tessa whispered. 'He could have been watching us all the evening!'

'Hm – probably! You should have told us Tessa. It might have been a valuable clue,' and he clicked his fingers and frowned thoughtfully.

'You . . . you mean they're using the tin-mines now . . . to store the cannabis?' Tessa asked excitedly, for the idea had come to her just now in the cove. Then she said with a shudder, 'Come on, David, let's get back,' for the incident was still very vivid in her mind and it was growing dusk.

'Yes, we'd better – though we're safe enough together,' he said, and they broke into a brisk walk, as they followed the narrow cliff-path. It seemed to Tessa that he had forgotten all about her for the minute, and was talking to himself as he went on, 'I've got to tell Dad . . . though I expect he and the police have guessed already, for I'm not told *everything* that's going on.' Then remembering Tessa again, he looked at her and grinned.

'*I* thought of that as soon as you told me about the whole thing just now,' Tessa said rather smugly, and David gave her a hearty slap on the back.

'Good old Tessa, what would we do without you?' he said, and she giggled as he went on, 'I *should* have thought of it and I don't know why I didn't – except that it was rather too obvious.'

'How do they get the cannabis here?' Tessa asked, for she had been puzzling about that at the back of her mind for the last half hour.

'By boat, we think, though we aren't sure . . .'

He broke off in mid-sentence, for they were nearing the little white-washed cottages on the headland now, and were surprised to see that Mr Jenkins was coming out of the gate and walking to meet them, quickening his footsteps as he drew nearer. Immediately Tessa saw his face, she knew something was wrong.

'The twins are missing!' Mr Jenkins told them as soon as he was within speaking distance, and he looked so serious that Tessa clapped her hand to her mouth and her face must have gone very white beneath her sunburn, for he went on, 'It's a bit worrying, but I'm sure everything will be all right and they'll turn up soon,' but she felt certain he was just trying to gloss over things to avoid alarming her. When she looked at David, she noticed that he too had turned rather pale, as his eyes met his father's.

'They went round to play with the Manners children this afternoon, I understand,' Mr Jenkins went on a little too brightly as he looked at Tessa again and she nodded silently, biting her lip, her mind racing ahead to all the alarming possibilities. 'Well, your Aunt was late getting back from Bodmin because unfortunately her car broke down and she had to take it into a garage for repair and catch a bus back, so she didn't get in until 6.30 – about half-an-hour ago.'

'Oh dear,' Tessa said flatly.

'Your Uncle was late coming home too, as he had been delayed at the office, and when he got in around six and the twins weren't there, he didn't think anything of it as he supposed they had gone with you as they had arranged last night. When your Aunt got back, she called round at the Manners – thinking the twins were still there – only to be told that they had left around five to go home. Of course, Mr and Mrs Manners had assumed that was where they were.'

They all stood silent and anxious for a moment, thinking hard, until Mr Jenkins went on, 'Your Uncle rang through here, wondering whether we had seen anything of them and fortunately I had just got in. I've searched the cliffs and beaches close by, but there's no sign of them, so we'll have to look further afield now.'

'Where *can* they be?' Tessa asked aghast, for surely they wouldn't have been so silly as to go wandering off on their own after that Sunday afternoon episode, even though it was the last day of the holidays and they felt like a final fling. But then she remembered that there hadn't been any fresh alarms for nearly three weeks now and the twins had probably almost forgotten that anything had ever happened.

They all started to walk back to the cottage then, and as they went Mr Jenkins squeezed Tessa's arm and told her again not to worry.

'They'll soon be found, I'm sure,' he said. 'We've been praying hard that they may be kept safe, wherever they are.'

But what he didn't tell Tessa and she didn't learn until afterwards was that Auntie and Uncle had already rung the police who were out scouring the cliffs and beaches within a thirty-mile radius, trying to trace the twins' whereabouts, for that would have made things look really grim.

Tessa cheered up a bit when Mr Jenkins said that, and they went indoors where Mrs Jenkins greeted them with a relieved smile, obviously glad to see Tessa back safe and sound. She bustled around the kitchen, making a pot of tea for them all and trying to look cheerful. After they had drunk it they all felt a bit better. Then Mr Jenkins said that the best thing they could do was to pray about it and commit it all to the Lord. So they all knelt down in the little sitting-room and Mr Jenkins prayed a simple prayer, asking for God's protection for Peter and Paula and that they might be brought safely back to them, and Tessa remembered the words of the chorus that had come down to her from the top of the cliff on the occasion of her first meeting with the smugglers. Perhaps the twins would be remembering them too, she thought, wherever they were, and would feel Jesus very close to them if they were in any sort of danger.

They got up from their knees and Mr Jenkins said, 'Come along, David, we'd better be going. You stay here with Mrs Jenkins, Tessa, until we have some news.'

But Tessa burst out pleadingly, 'Oh, please let me come too,' for he had already mentioned that Auntie and Uncle were out searching with Mr Trelawney, and the thought of having to stay behind whilst everyone else was out looking was too awful to contemplate.

'Well,' Mr Jenkins began rather dubiously, 'I don't know . . .'

But Tessa said again, 'Oh, *please* Mr Jenkins,' and he relented.

'You must keep close to us all the time though,' he warned, 'otherwise you'll be more of a liability than anything else,' and of course Tessa promised that she would.

'If Tessa's going, I'm coming too,' Mrs Jenkins said firmly, so after her husband had locked up securely, the five of them set off accompanied by Sheba.

'Was there any place the twins particularly liked or wanted to see badly?' Mr Jenkins asked as they swung off along the cliff-path, and Tessa frowned and thought hard for a moment. Then she stopped dead in her tracks, holding her breath and staring down at the ground.

'Yes,' she muttered, 'there was,' and everyone was looking at her and her heart started to thud, for as soon as Mr Jenkins had asked the question, there had flashed into her mind what Paula had said that very morning at breakfast. 'I'd love to see a tin-mine close to,' she had told Peter, and her pulses started to race at the remembrance, for supposing they had fallen down the shaft of one, or the smugglers had been around and nabbed them, and she didn't know which would be the worst.

So she told them what Paula had said and Mr and Mrs Jenkins looked thoughtful, whilst David shot Tessa a quick look. Then Mr Jenkins murmured quietly, 'Hm. We'd better go and look at the one on the headland.' So they changed direction and set off again. At least it was a good thing to have a definite object in view, instead of just wandering aimlessly.

It was getting dark as they came up over the headland

towards the tin-mine and they could see the outline of it, silhouetted eerily against the night sky. Tessa stared down towards the little cove, seeing the tossing waves glinting coldly in the inky blackness, and as she looked she saw to her surprise that the fishing boat was still there, though much further inshore than it had been earlier on in the evening.

'Look David,' she whispered, pointing to it and he frowned and looked puzzled and gave a low whistle of surprise. The next moment she heard a muffled sound on the rocks below. The others heard it too, and they all stood stock still and peered at one another in the darkness, whilst Mr Jenkins extinguished the beam of his powerful torch.

'There's something down there,' she gasped in a loud whisper, and she gripped Mrs Jenkins' arm with her cold fingers, the gaunt wall of the tin-mine towering above their heads close beside them. For Tessa had seen a man coming out of the sea with what looked like big tin boxes under each arm – what on earth could he be doing down there?

'Someone,' corrected Mr Jenkins grimly, 'and he's coming this way, by the look of things. Get down behind the wall love, and you too Tessa,' he ordered without looking round. 'And don't move, either of you, until I say so. Come on David, we're going to have to grab him when he gets up here.'

'Be careful, George,' Mrs Jenkins warned, as they both moved round to the back of the mine. They pressed their backs to the stonework, tense and anxious, and the next moment a small exclamation from David made them gasp and turn their heads. Then suddenly – unbelievably – the little cove was alive with people, and shadowy figures darted out from behind the rocks before their astonished gaze.

'The police!' David called softly. 'They've beaten us to it!' and ignoring another warning from Mr Jenkins to be careful, Tessa ran out from behind the wall, straining her eyes in the darkness to see what was happening.

'Police!' she echoed in amazement and Mrs Jenkins, who was close behind, whispered that the police were out looking for Peter and Paula. She hadn't realised that, of course, but she was thankful that they were there and that Mr Jenkins and David wouldn't have to tackle the man, whoever he was, on their own.

Tessa even forgot the twins in the excitement of what happened next, for they heard a muffled shout from down on the beach, followed by the sounds of a scuffle, and they could see figures rushing hither and thither over the sand. Then the man with the tin boxes had dropped them and was making a dash for it back into the sea, the police after him – and in a minute David, who with Mr Jenkins had hurried to the edge of the cliff to get a better view, called back that everything was under control and that they had snapped handcuffs on the man.

After that there was a little procession climbing the cliff-path towards them, and Tessa let out a big sigh of relief as she watched Mr Jenkins and David go forward to speak to the police – though they had signalled to the two of them first to keep close together, for as Mrs Jenkins whispered to her, there could be other smugglers around. After a few words, the little body of men, with their prisoner in the middle, passed them on the cliff path and made their way back in the direction of the village.

'An accomplice of the smugglers!' David told them excitedly. 'He brings the cannabis in every day by boat and sits out there all evening in the cove until it gets dark, pretending he's getting in lobster-pots. His name's Wilf Smith!'

'Our fisherman!' Tessa gasped astonished, and her thoughts flew back to earlier in the evening when they had seen the fishing-boat out in the bay and the 'fisherman' hauling in his pots – and to the other occasions when they had seen it too. Then she caught her breath, for there had been something familiar about the man too, and where had she seen him before, apart from out in the boat?

'Thank God they've got one of them anyway,' Mr Jenkins said, and Tessa remembered the twins – who hadn't been very far from her thoughts all the time, of course – and she asked Mr Jenkins whether the man the police had just caught might know something about their whereabouts.

'Well Tessa, they're hoping now to get some information that should help,' he told her. 'They've already searched the mine and there's no trace of them there – though there are a lot of tins of cannabis down at the bottom, as we anticipated. So I don't think there's anything more we can do at the moment because it's time you were in bed, and we ought to be getting you back home.'

So they turned in the direction of the coastguard cottages and David asked Tessa as they went whether she had been able to get a look at the man's face and if so whether he was perhaps the shorter of the two men who had haunted her.

'No, he isn't,' Tessa said puzzled, for she would have recognised either of them anywhere by now. 'But I *have* seen him before somewhere, I'm sure. Who . . . who is he?'

And Mr Jenkins said he could answer that one, for he had known him by his walk as soon as he had set eyes on him, for he had one leg slightly shorter than the other. He was a man who had moved into the village about two months before with an alsatian dog, and had rented a cottage there.

Tessa gasped then and said, 'I know where I saw him! He was on the beach at Poltuan one afternoon – just round the corner to the left where there's that little sandy cove. When you said about the alsatian I remembered, and he *did* have a limp, because I noticed it. He was the same man we saw near the coach that day at Dozmary Pool too, David, when the dog growled at Sheba!' she finished breathlessly. Then she looked quickly at Mr Jenkins and said, 'Do you think he was spying on us?' and her eyes grew round as saucers at the thought.

'Very likely,' Mr Jenkins said grimly. 'But he won't do it any more!'

By now they were back at the coastguard cottages and Mr Jenkins got out the car and drove Tessa home. But before she went, Mrs Jenkins kissed her and told her not to worry too much.

13: Tessa to the Rescue

Tessa couldn't help worrying though, and as soon as she got home and the twins weren't there—which she had been hoping against hope they might be—she burst into tears. Auntie and Uncle were both looking very tired and anxious, so she dried her eyes whilst Mr Jenkins told them about what had happened down at the cove. They cheered up a little after that, and Uncle said that perhaps there might be some news soon now.

After Mr Jenkins had said goodbye, Auntie gave Tessa a glass of hot milk, but although she was very tired, she didn't want to go to bed yet, and she guessed that Auntie and Uncle wouldn't either, until there was news of the twins. So she sipped her milk slowly until Auntie told her to drink up and go to bed, when she sighed and asked if she could stay up a little longer. But Uncle said no, she would be very tired in the morning if she didn't get some sleep, so she went reluctantly out of the room, and along the passage towards her bedroom. She had to pass Paula's room on the way, and she didn't quite know what made her do it, but on a sudden impulse she pushed open the door which was ajar, and looked inside.

The little room was quite tidy, for Paula always put her clothes and shoes away in the wardrobe, and didn't usually leave things lying about. Now, her case—ready packed but open—stood in the middle of the pink carpet, and as Tessa paused there for a moment, deep in thought, her eyes lighted suddenly on a screwed up piece of paper peeping out from behind the waste-paper basket almost at her feet.

So without thinking, she stooped and picked it up—and she was just about to drop it into the basket, when she changed her mind and straightened it out instead. There was a drawing on it of a little tumbled-down cottage—quite a good drawing too, for Paula drew well—and as she stared idly down at it, something rang a bell, and she had a sudden wave of inspiration, her thoughts winging back to that afternoon when Peter and Paula had gone missing, and had discovered the two little cottages which had held such a fascination for them.

This must be one of those cottages, Tessa guessed, and all at once—as an idea came into her head—she gave a gasp and her hand flew to her mouth. Perhaps the twins had gone there this evening for a last look! And as she continued to gaze at the drawing which had been carefully coloured with crayons, she was reminded of something Mr Jenkins had said earlier on and another idea struck her which nearly took her breath away. For he had told them that the man called Wilf Smith whom the police had just caught down in the cove, lived in one of two dilapidated cottages on the outskirts of the village. The twins' cottages, of course! Though not this one, the drawing of which she was holding in her hand—but the other one which Peter and Paula had said looked lived in.

The next minute Tessa was racing back along the passage to the dining-room, waving the piece of paper at Uncle and Auntie who were still sitting on the settee where she had left them, talking in uneasy undertones. And she knew—with sudden intuition—that they were wondering whether they ought to ring Mummy and Daddy now, to let them know about the twins, or whether they should wait a little longer in the hope that the police might ring with some good news. Their conversation stopped abruptly as she came through the door, and they both looked round, surprised.

'The little cottage!' she said jubilantly, without any preliminaries. 'Paula's done a drawing of it! I've just found it on her bedroom floor. She wanted to go back and have a look at it – they've both wanted to ever since they saw it that evening when they went out on their own and went down that lane and walked round the garden,' she explained breathlessly, the words tumbling out all of a jumble.

'What cottage?' Uncle asked in bewilderment, and Auntie got up quickly and took the piece of crumpled paper from her hand and studied it. Then they were both looking at her with puzzled frowns, for they had forgotten all about the cottages.

'Don't you see,' Tessa said impatiently, 'that's where they may have gone! For a last look at them before we go home!'

They both remembered then, and Auntie asked 'But where are the cottages?' whilst Uncle looked thoughtful. They were only about half-a-mile away, Tessa told them, and she knew where they were for the twins had pointed them out to her one day when they had been out on a walk with the Beach Mission.

Uncle got to his feet and glanced at Auntie.

'We'll go and have a look,' he said. 'At least it's better than sitting here doing nothing,' he murmured to her. So they all went into the hall to get their anoraks, and Uncle found a large torch. Then, after he had closed and locked the front door behind them, they set off.

It was raining now – a fine, steady drizzle – and Tessa remember thinking sadly to herself that the long hot summer was really at an end now, though it wasn't so bad really, because they were going home tomorrow. Then she pulled herself up short, realising suddenly that they wouldn't be going home tomorrow – at least the twins wouldn't, if they were still missing . . . and she fell to wondering whether she would be sent home on her own, and she did so hope that she wouldn't.

Then she told herself that she must stop being miserable, for God knew all about the twins and where they were, and He would take care of them. And the thought came to her that Mr and Mrs Jenkins and David would be praying for them all at that very moment, and after that she felt much calmer.

'You turn right,' Tessa said as they went out through the gate, 'and go along the road for a while, and then you turn right again by a Dutch barn. The cottages are a little way down the lane past the farm, on the left-hand side behind a tall hedge with a gap in it and no gate.'

'I wonder whether we ought to have told the police first,' Auntie said as they walked along the dark road, and Uncle replied that they probably ought, but it wasn't worth turning back now, and they would just go along and have a look. Then Tessa remembered that she hadn't told them that she was certain the man who had been caught tonight lived in one of the cottages, this vital piece of information having, for some inexplicable reason, entirely slipped her mind.

So she told them what Mr Jenkins had said. Auntie drew in her breath, and Uncle said nothing. Then they were turning the corner into the lane, and walking along it in silence, and Tessa was thinking about the big black alsatian, and knowing that she ought to have warned Uncle and Auntie about that too, but she had been afraid they might have refused to come if they knew about the dog. Besides which, Peter and Paula had said that it had been shut up in the other cottage. Though supposing it should happen to be loose tonight; her heart leapt into her throat at the thought!

It was too late to think about that now though, for they were there, and Tessa whispered, 'This is it!' and they stopped, Uncle switching off his torch. Then, under cover of darkness, they were peering anxiously through the gap in the hedge, and Tessa was praying very hard that they wouldn't be disappointed. Though what they expected to find she was not quite sure, except that the twins could have got locked in by accident, or perhaps left some clue to their whereabouts.

There were no lights in either cottage, and the longer they waited, the more obvious it seemed that there was no one there – twins or smugglers – for there was not a sound to be heard but the rain dripping off the trees, and the thumping of Tessa's heart, and she felt terribly disappointed as her hopes faded rapidly – though she knew they had really only been clutching at straws. In any case, it seemed likely that the police had already been there anyway, as Auntie pointed out to Uncle with a worried sigh.

Uncle however signalled to them to go forward, and Tessa's heart beat even faster as they crept up the little weed-covered path towards the empty cottage. At that moment there came a deep-throated growl from over to their right, and Tessa jumped and said, 'The dog! There's a – a big alsatian in there! I forgot to tell you,' Auntie said, 'Oh Tessa!' and they all three stood stockstill holding their breath. Then Uncle, his eyes fixed on one of the ground-floor windows of the other cottage, said, 'It's all right, he's shut up indoors,' and they all relaxed.

Tessa didn't think it any use to try the front door, for she remembered very clearly that the twins had said it was locked. So instead she went round to the left on her own, over the weed-covered lawn, and peered anxiously in through the dirty, cobweb-filled windows of the lower rooms for some sign of the twins, though she could hardly distinguish anything inside at all.

Then she went on round the back to the other side, and at first she couldn't think where Uncle and Auntie had got to, until she realised that the little side door stood open and they must actually be inside the cottage. Yet she was sure the twins had said that the side door had been locked too.

So she crept quickly through the little door and found herself in a dirty kitchen with a broken sink in the corner, an empty cupboard with the door hanging off its hinges, and hardly any other furniture except a rickety table in the middle of the floor. Uncle and Auntie were just coming out again to look for her, looking worried because they had just realised she wasn't with them, and Uncle put a warning finger to his lips as he crept back towards the inside door and turned the handle noiselessly. Then she and Auntie followed him through, and they were in a tiny hall with two other doors leading off it, and shabby linoleum on the floor.

Uncle opened each door in turn and they tip-toed after him and peered inside, but Tessa knew that the same thought was in all their minds, that it was quite hopeless. Uncle, however, pointed to the bare, narrow staircase leading to the first floor, beckoning them to follow him.

'We'll just go up and have a look,' he whispered over his shoulder, and they crept up the creaky, uncarpeted stairs, stepping on to a little square low-ceilinged landing at the top, where Uncle flashed his torch around, and they saw that there was a door facing them which was shut and one to the side which wasn't. Uncle immediately went towards the low doorway of the latter, bending his head as he went through, and Tessa and Auntie followed, Tessa feeling ready to drop with tiredness and disappointment.

Then suddenly Uncle murmured something under his breath which Tessa didn't catch, and she saw him move forward and stand stockstill, staring down at the floor in the left-hand corner of the room. And when she and Auntie crept over to see what had caught his attention, they noticed that one of the floorboards had been taken up and put back again – though not properly, for it was sticking up a bit at one end.

Next minute, Uncle was down on his knees, peering at something underneath the board, and when Tessa stared over his shoulder, holding her breath, she saw to her amazement that there were a lot of shiny tin boxes stacked beneath the boards, and without thinking, she shouted 'Cannabis' out loud, and promptly clapped her hand to her mouth, as Uncle gave her a warning frown.

Meanwhile Auntie was gazing at Uncle with a puzzled, startled expression on her face, and then Uncle was straightening up, and it was at that moment that Tessa heard a faint sound!

They all heard it in fact – a little scuffle on the other side of the wall which caused Tessa to draw in her breath sharply and go stiff all over, her thoughts flying at once to rats! And then it came again, a little louder this time, and unbelievably, Paula's piping voice came to them quite clearly, though a little muffled-sounding, through the thickness of the wall.

Tessa's heart gave a great leap of joy then, and Uncle was looking at Auntie, and all their faces were shining with incredulity and relief. For a long moment they stood absolutely still and silent, holding their breath and staring at one another wide-eyed.

'Wake up Peter, for goodness' sake! It's so dark and – and creepy.'

It was Paula's voice again, sounding a little stronger though still indistinct, and there was an unmistakeable sob in it. '*I* can't sleep, even if you can! These horrid bare boards! Oh . . . I'm s-so s-stiff and c-cold, and I d-do w-wish we'd never come!'

All three came alive then, and Uncle was on the landing in a trice, Auntie and Tessa close on his heels. Next minute he was tugging at the door-handle and rattling it as though he intended to break the door down. Though it was locked, of course, and the twins were both calling out in frightened, angry voices, 'Let us out! Please let us out! You've no right to keep us here.'

'It's all right, darlings,' Auntie said soothingly. 'It's us – Uncle and Auntie and Tess,' whilst Uncle added, 'We'll have you out in no time, twins.'

Though all Tessa managed was, 'Hello twins,' in a faint whisper, because she was quite overwhelmed by it all.

Then Auntie was looking at Uncle anxiously, and asking him what he thought they ought to do, and Uncle was flashing his torch around the landing and walking briskly back to the other room. Next minute Tessa heard him call out, 'That's lucky! They've dropped the key just in under the floorboard. They must have left in a hurry!'

'Yes, they did!' shouted Peter who was obviously wide awake now and fully aware of what was happening, and Paula asked excitedly, 'How did you find us?'

'It's all thanks to Tess,' Auntie told them, and Uncle said, 'Yes, well done Tess!' and patted her on the shoulder.

By now he had fitted the key into the lock and turned it, and then the door was wide open and they were looking into another dirty, bare little room festooned with cobwebs. There were some old rugs spread over the middle of the floor, on which the twins had obviously been sleeping, but now Paula was hurling herself into Auntie's arms and sobbing – with relief this time, whilst Peter gave a huge yawn and a sigh, and looked a bit guilty as well.

'Come along children, we're going home now,' Uncle told them cheerfully, 'and you can tell us all about it when we're well away from this place. Don't make a sound because we don't want the dog to start barking again.'

They crept down the creaking staircase to the ground floor, and Tessa was hoping and praying that the men would not return and find them there. For this cottage, she now knew beyond a shadow of doubt, was the smugglers' headquarters – next door to the one where the third man lived, and it was also used for storing some of the cannabis.

They went noiselessly through the kitchen and out into the garden. It was still raining a little, though not so heavily. They looked all round cautiously, but there was no sign of anybody or anything, so they set off down the pathway towards the gap in the hedge, and just as they reached it there came the sound of a car being driven rapidly along the lane, followed by a furious barking from one of the front windows of the other cottage.

Uncle bundled everyone quickly into the shadow of the tall hedge, and put an arm round each of the twins, whilst Tessa clung to Auntie; there they stood, pressed into the rain-sodden bushes amongst the shadows, scarcely daring to breathe and certain that the men had returned. The twins, terrified all over again, stared up at Uncle, whilst Tessa bit her lip hard and looked nervously at Auntie.

Next minute there came a clatter of footsteps in the lane, and the sound of men's voices – and all at once they each of them knew, with an overwhelming sense of relief, that everything was all right and that it was the police who had arrived!

They relaxed then and came out from hiding, and Uncle was walking through the gap to speak to the four uniformed men standing in the middle of the muddy lane near the big police car, flashing their torches around and murmuring in undertones to each other.

'We've found them!' Uncle announced in a matter-of-fact sort of voice, and Tessa couldn't help smiling to herself at the astonished expressions on the policemen's faces when they turned round and saw them all, particularly the twins.

'Peter and Paula here were locked in one of the top rooms of the left-hand cottage,' Uncle told them, nodding back over his shoulder, 'and you'll find some tin boxes under a loose floorboard in the other room that might interest you too,' he added grimly.

The policemen nodded briskly, in command of the situation once more, and glanced quickly through the hedge towards the cottages, and back again to the weary, though radiant faces of the group before them.

'You beat us to it then!' remarked one of them with a smile, and Tessa said quickly, 'You haven't found the other two smugglers yet, have you?' much too excited to feel in awe of the law, and certain that she could never feel afraid of anyone or anything ever again after all that had happened.

'Not yet, my dear!' said another of the men, smiling down at Tessa's eager face, 'But rest assured, we shall before long.'

'Good work anyway, Sir,' said the Sergeant to Uncle. 'We'd an idea the children might be here, and came straight over after questioning the chap we picked up in the cove earlier on. He lives in the right-hand cottage, and he keeps a fierce alsatian, by the sound of it, to keep away intruders. The other two must have scarpered, but we'll pick 'em up before long,' he added cheerfully.

Then the police were questioning the twins, and Peter and Paula were explaining rather sheepishly how they came to be in the cottage in the first place.

Paula said, 'It was the last evening you see, and we did so want to see the cottages again,' and Peter added defensively that they hadn't seen any harm.

'And then what?' asked the Sergeant, his face expressionless as he scribbled rapidly in his notebook.

'We came here and started looking round the garden. Then we found the side door was open so we . . . we went in and up the stairs,' Paula said nervously.

'We went into one of the rooms,' Peter chipped in, 'and there was a loose floorboard – and when we looked we saw something underneath. We were just standing there, when two men came up the stairs carrying big tin boxes, and they dragged us into the other room and locked the door on us,' he said, turning pale beneath his sunburn at the thought of it.

'We've been there ages,' Paula said tearfully, her wet, bedraggled hair falling all over her face, 'and it was freezing and f-filthy, and ... and th-they never brought us any food.'

'Only threw in an old rug for us to sit on because there were bare boards,' said Peter, torn between feeling something of a hero and a bit foolish at the same time.

'Did they say anything to you?' was the next question and Paula thought for a moment and told him all they had said was, 'Got you at last, you plaguey children. We'll teach you to snoop on us – and that sister of yours!' Then she wrinkled her nose in bewilderment and asked, 'Whatever did they mean?'

'We knew who they were though,' Peter butted in quickly. 'They were those horrid men in the churchyard!'

'Right! Did they say anything else to you?' asked the Sergeant, still scribbling.

'No! We shouted and screamed and kicked the door, but they didn't take any notice,' said Peter, who was beginning to enjoy all the attention – though Paula was starting to cry in real earnest now.

'They came back later on,' she sobbed, 'and they s-seemed in-in a t-terrible hurry. I ... I think they were t-taking out th-the t-tin b-boxes again.'

'And carrying them downstairs,' Peter said, wide-eyed with excitement.

'It w-was p-pitch black,' said Paula recovering herself a little, 'a-and we were ever so frightened. They kept running up and downstairs and ... and shouting and telling each other that the game was all up and they had b-better get out and leave the rest of the s-stuff.'

'And then they went,' Peter finished, 'and it was absolutely horrid.'

'That would be when we picked up Wilf Smith down in the cove,' put in one of the policemen. 'They had obviously got wind of it. Now all we've got to do is to find them, for our friend back at the station has told us their names and all we want to know about them. They've been living in a gypsy caravan further up the lane for the past few weeks.'

Then Uncle said they absolutely must go home and if the police wanted any more information they could ring him. Whereupon the Sergeant said, 'Jump in, and I'll run you all back, Sir,' and he opened the car doors for them. Then they were being driven swiftly back along the narrow lane and homewards, leaving the other three policemen behind to search the cottage.

'Whatever are they going to do about the alsatian?' Tessa asked anxiously, remembering how it had sprung towards her in the cove that afternoon, but Uncle told her they would know how to deal with that.

As soon as they arrived back home, Auntie bundled Tessa and the twins into bed with hot-water bottles, bringing them milk and biscuits to send them off to sleep. They could lie in next morning for as long as they liked, she told them, for they wouldn't be going back home the next day if they didn't feel like it.

Peter and Paula were soon asleep, but Tessa lay awake for ages, re-living the events of the last few hours. And when finally she did drop off, it was to dream that smugglers were chasing the three of them over the cliffs towards the tin-mine, and that she was falling, falling, into space!

Then after that, she dropped off into a deep, dreamless slumber.

14: Home Again

It was nearly ten o'clock before Tessa awoke next morning, and as soon as she opened her eyes everything came flooding back and she jumped out of bed and ran to the window, wide awake and excited. Though as she drew back the curtains and the realisation dawned that it was the very last time she would see that panorama of fields, cliffs and sea — at least for quite a long while — she felt a pang of sadness.

There wasn't time to brood about it though, for next minute the twins came bouncing noisily into her bedroom in their dressing-gowns, yawning and rubbing the sleep out of their eyes after their late night. They seemed in good spirits however, and none the worse for their adventure, and were full of questions of course, which she did her best to answer — though she couldn't answer all of them. Then they dressed quickly and went downstairs to the dining-room where a big breakfast awaited them.

They tucked in with gusto — particularly the twins who had missed their supper the previous evening — and whilst they were eating, the front door bell rang, after which, by the sound of the voices, they knew that the Jenkins had arrived. So they finished their meal and went into the lounge where not only the Jenkins — with Sheba, of course — but Mr Trelawney too, were sitting chatting to Uncle, who was looking a bit weary, though very cheerful.

It was the first time the children had seen their rescuer, the detective, since their ordeal in the churchyard, and he got up and greeted them with a handshake and a cheerful smile, saying how pleased he was to see his young friends again – and all safe and well.

The Jenkins too were looking delighted, and Mr Jenkins said that they had been so relieved to get the telephone call around midnight with the news that the twins were found.

'None of us would have slept a wink otherwise, I'm sure,' Mrs Jenkins added, 'for we were all so worried!'

Then they were all chattering at once, reliving the night's adventures, and Mr Trelawney filled them in with all the bits they didn't know about, whilst David told Tessa he thought it had been very clever of her to think of that bright idea about the little cottages – not to mention her other bright ideas, he teased. And rather to Tessa's surprise, she found herself coming in for a lot of congratulation.

So she pointed out modestly that even if she and Uncle and Auntie hadn't discovered the twins' whereabouts, the police would have found them very soon afterwards, but Mr Trelawney said the smugglers might just have decided to come back and take the twins off somewhere else a bit further away, and it was a good thing they had gone there as soon as possible.

As to Wilf Smith, the police had had their eye on him for some time, for when he wasn't away fetching the cannabis, he was wandering around the village and further afield with his big fierce dog. They had found him lurking on the beaches in a suspicious manner more than once. Now, putting two and two together, they guessed that the three smugglers, realising that it would be unsafe for Josh Brown and Jake Sharp to be seen around too much in daylight after their meeting with Tessa in the caves, had left it to Wilf to keep an eye on her. Though it had undoubtedly been Josh Brown whom she had seen standing by the tin mine on the night of the barbecue.

Last night, Mr Trelawney went on, the smugglers'

accomplice had sat out in the boat as usual until well past the time when his two friends usually appeared. When they didn't show up, he had realised there must be some hold-up which could spell trouble. He had then decided to land the boxes and stow them away in the mine on his own, by which time he had hoped the other two might turn up. Needless to say, he very much regretted not having made a quick get-away while the going was good!

The children listened to these details with great interest, particularly the twins who knew hardly anything at all of what had been going on, and whose eyes grew round as saucers in sheer amazement at the mere mention of the words 'smugglers' and 'cannabis', their excitement at fever pitch!

Mr Trelawney also cleared up one small point which had been puzzling the police and Mr Jenkins, and that was how it was that the police had not discovered the cannabis in Wilf Smith's boat before – for all the fishing boats and other local craft – including his – had been thoroughly searched at some time or another. Everything had been revealed last night however, when the tins of cannabis were found underneath the boat, attached by ropes tied to the hull, so that they would trail along underwater, completely hidden from view.

Of course, Mr Trelawney, as well as the police, had been in regular touch with Auntie and Uncle ever since Tessa's narrow escape on the beach, for her description of the two men and their strange behaviour had aroused their suspicions – which explained why the children's detective friend had known all about them and where they lived, that afternoon in the churchyard. He had turned up there quite by chance that Sunday afternoon, arriving soon after they did, having come with the intention of taking a look at the tomb, Mr Trelawney told them. After that frightening episode, the detective had warned Auntie and Uncle that it would be unsafe for Tessa and the twins to go anywhere on their own any more, and the beach party leaders had been alerted too, as Tessa had guessed.

Uncle and Auntie had even been advised that it might be best to send the three of them back to London should anything else of a startling nature occur. And how glad Tessa was that it hadn't, though it had been a very worrying time for everybody.

All that remained now was to pick up the other two men, and the police hoped it wouldn't be too long before they did that.

It was to be sooner than any of them expected though, for just as Mr Trelawney said that he must be going on, the telephone rang and when Uncle came back from answering it, his face wore a relieved smile. For it had been good news and the police had just rung to say that Josh Brown and Jake Sharp had been caught down at Fowey on the south coast half-an-hour before, where they had fled last night. Though the police had apparently only been just in time, for the two had been on the point of boarding a boat for France when they caught up with them, so that was another thing to be thankful for!

Now it really was time to say 'goodbye', so everyone went out to the gate to see their friend, the detective, off, and Mr Trelawney shook hands again all round before getting into his big white Cortina. How pleased he was to have met them all, he said, and how glad that everything had turned out well in the end – he hoped it hadn't spoilt the children's holiday too much, and that they would come back again next year. Tessa assured him that they would, and they all thanked him for looking after them so well and waved until his car disappeared from sight round a bend in the road.

Then the moment had come for the Jenkins to take their leave, and Tessa hugged Sheba, whilst David teased the twins and told them not to get into any more scrapes – and Tessa too, for that matter! Tessa said, on behalf of all three – for Peter and Paula were still so busy chattering about smugglers and cannabis, they couldn't think of anything else! – that they would certainly be coming to Cornwall next summer, all being well – if not before.

Then the Jenkins got into their car, Sheba bounding in onto the back seat, and they waved to their friends left standing on the pavement, until they turned into the lane leading to the cliffs, and couldn't see them any more.

After that, Uncle went to get his car out of the garage, for he was going to drive Tessa and the twins to the station to catch their train, and Auntie was coming too, to see them off. As soon as they had put the luggage into the boot, they piled in and were away, but before they left the village behind, Tessa turned round for a last glimpse of the cliffs, and caught sight of the little church standing amongst the tomb-stones. She could just see the three white-washed cottages on the headland beyond too – and she thought again of the smugglers, and felt so glad that they were caught! What a lovely holiday it had been though, in spite of it all, and what a lot there would be to tell Daddy and Mummy when they got home. The twins would never stop talking, she was sure.

Then she remembered the letter she had received from Sally yesterday, in which she had said that she had been in touch with her friend, the Bible Class leader, who was looking forward to meeting Tessa and the twins when the class started again after the holidays. Steve and she hoped that Peter and Paula were fit and flourishing, and that she herself was safe and well, and enjoying the remainder of her holiday – and they both looked forward to seeing all three of them again next year.

By that time they were at the station, and only just in time for the train was waiting. Uncle found them a compartment and he and Auntie gave them all a hug and a kiss before they climbed in. Then the train gave a jolt and they were moving; and the children got out their handkerchiefs and waved from the window until they were out of the station and couldn't see Uncle and Auntie any more.

The twins settled down with their comics as the train gathered speed, whilst Tessa in her corner seat got out the letter she had received from Melanie that very morning and re-read it. What would her friend say, Tessa wondered, when she wrote to her with all the latest news? Yet how glad she would be to learn that she and the twins were all right and that the smugglers had been caught at last! She had been thinking about them every day, she said, and praying hard that God would look after them all.

And He had, of course, Tessa thought happily as the train sped on its way, and He would go on doing so – for she was building on the rock now, and not upon the sand.

If you wish to receive *regular information* about *new books*, please send your name and address to:

London Bible Warehouse
PO Box 123
Basingstoke
Hants RG23 7NL

Name _____

Address _____

_____

_____

_____

I am especially interested in:
- [ ] Biographies
- [ ] Fiction
- [ ] Christian living
- [ ] Issue related books
- [ ] Academic books
- [ ] Bible study aids
- [ ] Children's books
- [ ] Music
- [ ] Other subjects

P.S. If you have ideas for new Christian Books or other products, please write to us too!